# BUSINESS BEFORE PLEASURE

## NATASHA GRACE

First Edition Published in March 2021

Second Edition Published in June 2021

ISBN: 978-1-955895-00-2

# CHAPTER ONE

Butterflies fluttered in Olivia Montgomery's stomach as she made her way across the lobby of Montgomery Hotels' headquarters. She'd just returned from checking on the refurbishment plans for the company's Boston hotel and, with that out of the way, was eager to follow up on the proposal she'd sent to her dad about opening a hotel near Yosemite National Park.

They'd spoken a little about it before she'd left. He'd quizzed her about the park's attendance, other hotels in the area, and options for employee lodging. It'd been the first time he'd ever shown interest in one of her many proposals, and she couldn't help but think that this was the one he'd finally approve.

And perhaps after she'd been given the chance to prove herself with this hotel, she'd get the opportunity to revisit some of her previously rejected proposals. There was one in particular she was keen on. A few other ideas had occurred to her, ways to make the property stand out…

She smiled as she stepped into the open elevator. She hadn't even gotten the green light for her Yosemite hotel yet and here she was thinking about what would come next!

Realistically, she understood that she still had a long way to go before her dreams came to fruition, but she couldn't contain her excitement. She'd been looking for ways to make her mark on the family business ever since she'd joined four years ago, and it looked as if things were finally going her way.

The elevator doors were closing when she saw a dark-haired man in a suit approaching, and quickly pressed the open button. "Sorry." She'd been so distracted she hadn't seen him.

"That's all right. Thanks," the handsome man said as he flashed her a smile and walked into the elevator.

"Sure."

She waited a second and when he didn't pick a floor, she asked, "What floor?"

He nodded at the panel. "The same—twelve."

She frowned as the metallic doors closed. It was just a little past seven in the morning. Only her father and a handful of other people were at the office right now, which was why she'd come in this early. She'd wanted a chance to talk with her father before everyone else arrived.

"Are you here to see Tom?" she asked. Tom Nichols was one of their most aggressive salespeople and was constantly reaching out to companies about hosting their corporate events at Montgomery hotels, but he usually came in later. A lot later.

"No. I'm here to see Victor Montgomery. The name's Adam Campbell," he said as he offered his hand.

He had an appointment with her dad? Dammit. She should've checked his schedule yesterday, but he rarely had morning meetings. These early hours were often the only time in his tightly scheduled day he had to focus on work uninterrupted. She guessed she'd just have to wait until he was free to talk to him about her proposal. Shoving her disappointment aside, she shook Adam's hand. "Olivia Montgomery."

"You're Victor's daughter," he said as he released her hand.

She nodded and it was then that she recognized the man's name. Adam was a real estate developer and part of the family who owned Dannier, the cosmetics company that made the facial cream her cousin liked so much.

"You want us to manage a hotel?" she guessed. In addition to operating their own hotels, Montgomery Hotels also managed properties on behalf of others. She'd heard about Adam building hotels, but had thought they were all low- to mid-range properties as opposed to the luxury ones Montgomery specialized in.

"You get right down to business, don't you?" He smiled as he nodded at her. "I'm buying The Mansion. The deal should be finalized in a day or two."

Liv's heart skipped a beat. The Mansion was the first hotel her grandfather had built. It'd originally been an office building that had served as the headquarters for the family's bank. After the bank moved to its current location in Midtown, her grandfather had converted the former offices into the ideal hotel, bringing together the most magnificent architectural features of some of the grandest castles in Europe. The family's bank had been his duty, but The Mansion had been his passion. He'd spent every moment he could spare there, pouring all his energy into operating the most luxurious, customer-focused hotel he could and had even filled in at the front desk a time or two when they were short-staffed.

Unfortunately, he'd been forced to sell it in the eighties to raise the funds needed to save the family bank, but he'd never forgotten it. He'd always regaled her and her brother with stories of his time there, recounting funny incidents with famous guests, reminiscing about overseeing the renovation, and describing the lavish parties they'd hosted.

He'd put his all into the hotel and hadn't been able to stay away—even after they'd sold it, much to her father's chagrin. Grandpa would occasionally have a drink in the bar or have lunch in the terrace room. He and Grandma had even snuck Olivia into the tearoom for high tea a couple times before Dad had found out and forbidden it.

The first proposal she'd ever sent to her dad had been to reacquire the property and, though Dad had rejected the proposal, she'd always planned to revisit the idea when she was more experienced. Simply put, The Mansion belonged with the family. And though she knew owning the hotel wouldn't bring Grandpa back, she wanted to do right by his memory.

Fate, it seemed, had other plans.

"I wasn't aware Quinley was selling," she said, referring to the multinational company who currently owned The

Mansion. They hadn't been when she'd pitched her proposal to her dad two years ago, but she'd suspected they would sell at the right price. Since they'd never properly refurbished the hotel, it was doubtful they'd had any intention to hold the property for the long term.

She wondered how much Adam was paying for The Mansion and tamped down the urge to ask him if he'd be willing to sell the hotel outright to Montgomery. Not only would she be stepping way beyond her role in the company —especially without talking to her dad first—but it simply wouldn't do to sound too eager. The estimated price tag of The Mansion was one of the reasons her father had given her for his refusal. But the real estate market wasn't as hot now as it had been then. The property would be considerably cheaper.

"It's being used as part of their settlement to pay off some debt," Adam said. "I know that it's going to take a lot of renovation to bring it up to standard, but I think it's going to be a fine hotel when it's done."

*A fine hotel? A lot of renovation?*

What the hell was he talking about? All the hotel needed was an upgrade to modernize some of the mechanical and electrical facilities and perhaps an updated interior design. There had been a lot of maintenance neglected over the years, but she'd always thought it one of the most visually stunning hotels she'd ever seen. With its glass-covered atrium and marble columns, it had a classic, almost timeless, beauty few could rival. She could easily see it being one of the top New York City hotels again with just a little bit of work.

"What kind of renovations were you thinking about?" she asked, hoping her voice sounded even and not defensive about the suggestion that The Mansion was substandard. Thankfully, he didn't seem to notice.

"Some updating and light restoration to the exterior and then pretty much gutting the interior common floors for something more welcoming and less pretentious."

*He wanted to gut the inside?*

Her ears rang as she thought about the gorgeous lobby with its painted ceilings and sweeping double staircase being demolished. How dare he call it pretentious? It wasn't pretentious, it was Old-World charm and sophistication. Its stately features conjured the elegance of eras past that made you feel as if you'd been transported in time. Oh, and the ballroom!

The man simply had no taste if he wanted to wreck it.

"Completely revamping the tearoom," he continued. "Moving the bar to make room for a bigger restaurant, consolidating the rooms into bigger rooms and residences..."

A sense of foreboding crept into her as she recognized the excitement in Adam's eyes. It hadn't only been the potential costs that had made her dad reject her proposal. He'd thought the hotel needed a major facelift and had basically said that her judgment had been clouded by her grandfather's "tales of old."

What if Adam's plans for a major renovation lined up with what Dad thought and Dad agreed to manage the hotel? Instead of being happy that The Mansion would be under Montgomery's management again, Olivia would weep at the loss of the very essence of her grandfather's hotel.

The Mansion had been Grandpa's life. He'd labored over every square inch of the design of the hotel, right down to hand-selecting most of the materials used. If Grandpa wasn't already dead, hearing about Adam's plans to destroy what he'd built would surely kill him.

The elevator doors opened to their reception area and Adam laughed. "I'm sorry. I always get caught up in the excitement of the early stages of a project."

With Adam being so invested in The Mansion already, it seemed unlikely he'd be willing to sell the hotel to them. He'd want to see the renovation through. Her head pounded as she forced out a comment. "No. I understand."

She just prayed she'd read him wrong and that her dad would offer him a deal he couldn't resist. Though Dad had rejected her proposal, she doubted he'd stand idly by and allow Adam to basically demolish the hotel that meant so much to the family.

She headed towards the receptionist, Carol, who looked up with a smile.

"Hey, Olivia! Welcome back."

"Thanks, Carol. Will you please let Paula know Adam Campbell's here to see my dad?" she asked as she tilted her head in Adam's direction.

Carol's eyes widened as she glanced his way. "Hi," she said breathlessly and Olivia bit back a smile. Carol was a sucker for handsome men and Adam was definitely handsome. Too bad he wanted to destroy her grandfather's hotel.

"Hello." His voice was laced with amusement.

Carol shook herself out of the spell and picked up her phone.

"Thanks," Olivia mouthed and turned to Adam. "It was nice meeting you," she said as she shook his hand.

"Yeah. You, too."

Wondering about how Adam's discussion with her dad would go, Olivia headed to her office to regroup. After being out of town, she had a lot to catch up on, but given what was happening with The Mansion, there was no way she'd be able to concentrate.

"Oh, Liv. I forgot." She turned and saw Carol approaching her with message slips in her hand. "The head chef in San Antonio quit and Gary Bruning is worried that Maxwell is poaching our staff in San Diego."

Olivia sighed as she took the messages. "Thanks." As the relations manager for Montgomery's franchisees, she was constantly dealing with small crises like these. The problems were almost always urgent, but they weren't necessarily issues that demanded a specific knowledge base or skill set. They were problems pretty much anyone could solve.

So while her job was important, it didn't always feel meaningful, which was one of the main reasons why she kept submitting proposals to her dad even though he kept rejecting them. She wanted to create something, too, and to help grow Montgomery Hotels the way her father had. Montgomery Hotels' portfolio had only consisted of six hotels when he'd taken over and now it had just under forty. Her dreams weren't as big, but she wanted to contribute something to the family legacy.

As she settled at her desk, she made a mental note to ask Paula to call her as soon as her father was available so that she could talk to him about her proposal. Then she'd quiz him about The Mansion to see what his intentions were.

If Montgomery did end up managing it, she'd campaign to save as much of her grandfather's original design as possible. Given Adam's and Dad's views, an outright restoration seemed out of the question, but perhaps they could reach a compromise where they retained some of the characteristics that made the hotel so special, like the hand-painted ceilings and the gilt moldings.

But doubt remained. Adam had seemed pretty excited about revamping the hotel. How open to preserving anything could he actually be if he was already planning to gut the place?

Perhaps he wouldn't want such drastic changes if she could show him alternate designs that combined the modern aesthetic he was aiming for with all the characteristics that made The Mansion so special…

She'd start reviewing potential architects immediately. She'd need to find an architect who specialized in refreshing older buildings—one who could appease Adam's desire of modernization while still being true to The Mansion. A couple of firms came to mind and she pulled up their files to dig deeper.

If the deal went through, she wanted to have an architect at the ready. She couldn't give anyone the opportunity to submit a competing proposal that would destroy what her grandfather had created.

She'd already let her grandfather's memory down once. She wasn't about to do so again.

* * *

"Would you be willing to sell the hotel outright to us?" Victor Montgomery asked after listening to Adam's proposal. "I'm sure we can reach a deal that would be beneficial to the both of us."

"I doubt we could settle on a price that would satisfy the both of us," Adam said honestly. He didn't want to waste time with negotiations he knew would be futile. He had absolutely no intention of selling The Mansion. "With the renovation, The Mansion's value could easily quadruple in a few years and I wouldn't accept a valuation that reflected any less than that." Montgomery might be willing to pay a premium for the hotel, but he very much doubted they'd be willing to base their price on projected earnings.

"Then how about a partnership?"

Adam shook his head. "I'm only looking for an operator to manage the hotel." He never shared ownership in any of his developments, always preferring to either use his own money or, as in this case, to borrow.

After living under his parents' thumbs, he enjoyed the freedom of doing what he wanted without anyone else dictating what he could or couldn't do. He knew he'd be able to expand AC Developments more quickly if he allowed investors into his projects, but he didn't want to be beholden to anyone but himself.

He'd been prepared to make some concessions in order to work with Montgomery—like, perhaps a higher fee schedule or a longer contract period—but to give up equity when he didn't have to? Absolutely not.

"Then I think it's best you find another operator," Victor replied. "As I'm sure you're aware, Montgomery doesn't compete with our franchisees in the same marketplace. The income from operating the hotel simply wouldn't make up for the opportunity cost of not having our own hotel in New York."

Adam's jaw tightened. The fact that Montgomery didn't have a hotel in New York had been one of the reasons he'd approached them. It was a common occurrence for an operator to manage competing hotels in the same city, but he wanted better for The Mansion. It deserved to be the sole focus of its operator, at least in the region.

Montgomery had had a hotel in New York a few years ago but had sold their shares to their partner. He didn't know exactly what had happened but had heard Gen Capital, their partner at the time, had gotten involved in lawsuits for manipulating their finances since then.

He should've known Montgomery would want to own the hotel when they entered New York again. It was one thing to manage hotels for others, and quite another to do so when it was on your own turf. It was probably why they hadn't rushed into opening another property. They'd wanted to take their time and do things right.

The Mansion would be the same for him. He'd had a lot

of success in other real estate markets but had never dipped his toes into New York's even though he lived here. And now that he had The Mansion, he was pulling out all the stops. It would be the project he'd see and visit the most and he was willing to pay a premium to ensure its success.

Furthermore, he wanted to show his parents how far he'd come. Since The Mansion was just two blocks from Dannier's headquarters, they'd see it every time they headed to the office. It was petty of him, but he loved the idea of rubbing his success in their faces. He was well aware that they hated his success—hated not having a part of it. They'd expected him to come crawling back after they'd cut him off and instead, he was building an empire that would soon outgrow theirs.

Even better, The Mansion was a favorite venue of the old-money crowd for their parties—parties his parents wanted to attend but were never invited to. And soon, he'd own the hotel. It was almost too good to believe.

But was he willing to give up a portion of The Mansion in order to work with Montgomery? Considering the determination in Victor's eyes, Adam guessed that a partnership might be the only way Victor would agree to manage the hotel.

And Adam really wanted The Mansion to be a Montgomery Hotel. On top of the company being consistently ranked as a customer favorite, it was owned by the legendary Montgomery family. Even if it was just for business, he'd do what his parents had never been able to do— rub shoulders with old money.

"I'd be willing to form a partnership," he finally agreed.

It wasn't what he'd originally intended, but he couldn't deny that there'd be benefits he hadn't fully considered. In addition to lessening his financial exposure, the partnership would guarantee Montgomery had a vested interest in the project's success. Though they had a reputation for being straight shooters, it didn't hurt to ensure their management decisions benefited the hotel for the long term.

Victor hesitated before nodding. "All right. Send me the financials as well as the current franchise and tenant agreements, and we'll put together an offer. Are you looking for anything in particular in regards to the renovation?"

"I have ideas, but nothing concrete." He'd considered hiring the architect he'd used for his shopping complexes before crossing off the idea. While he had no complaints about Clarke's work, he knew that Clarke's forte was with new buildings—not renovating historic ones. Montgomery would undoubtedly have a better sense of who to hire for this kind of project.

"I don't want to touch the exterior except for some light restoration," he continued. The unique façade incorporated a traditional aesthetic that was rarely seen in the city these days. In fact, he was surprised the building hadn't been designated as a historical landmark yet. Not only had the property seen its fair share of history, but it had also been the venue for many important weddings and political events. "But I wouldn't mind gutting the interior in favor of something more contemporary, perhaps something similar to what you did in Los Angeles." That hotel had a modern design that came off as both classy and inviting.

"You've seen the renovated hotel?"

"Yes. I had a meeting at the restaurant inside last year and really loved the design."

Victor laughed. "I'll let my daughter know. I didn't agree with the concept, but she was most adamant." Adam wondered if he was talking about Olivia but refrained from asking. He didn't want to give the man any reason to back away from the project.

Victor tapped the folder Adam had brought in. "Now, how about the leases on the store tenants?" he asked, referring to the boutique stores on the ground floor and Adam guessed that Victor was thinking of replacing the tenants with higher-end ones. The Mansion had once housed some of the most exclusive brands in the world, but as the hotel's quality declined over the years, so had the stores'.

"We have the option to buy out the leases early. Do you have other tenants in mind?"

Victor confirmed Adam's suspicions by throwing out the names of a few high-end brands to approach and that launched a discussion about the overall strategy for the retail spaces in terms of square footage and the number of tenants to target.

Victor had some clear ideas about how to keep the balance between exclusivity and maximizing profit per square foot without compromising the overall customer experience, being mindful that it wasn't just the hotel guests who shopped at the stores, but the general public as well.

The more Victor talked, the more Adam liked the idea of having a business partner like him. Victor was the kind of man who clearly valued not only the bottom line, but the customer's experience as well. It was no wonder Montgomery had such a loyal customer base.

"I'll have my guys contact yours," Victor said as he walked Adam out of the meeting room thirty minutes later, and Adam knew he'd made the correct decision to attend the meeting alone.

Adam doubted the meeting would've gone as well if he'd shown up with an army of advisors. Victor seemed the old-fashioned type—someone who made business deals based on his own instincts, then let the negotiators and lawyers work out all the details.

"Great. I look forward to hearing from them." And he'd do what he could to move the deal along on his end. Not only would having a hotel operator in place as soon as possible bring more legitimacy to the project, it would also ease the transition process when ownership changed hands.

As they walked towards the lobby, Adam caught a glimpse of Olivia in her office, her head bent as she worked. The urge to go and talk with her surprised him. They'd only spoken briefly in the elevator, but she'd made an impression. He wasn't sure if it was her straight-to-business questions or her interest in The Mansion, but she'd just been so easy to talk with.

He silently laughed at himself. Did he really need to make excuses for wanting to approach a beautiful woman? Still, it might be awkward veering towards her office with her dad guiding him towards the elevators.

He'd talk to her the next time he visited. He'd make sure of it.

# CHAPTER TWO

It was close to five when Olivia finally made her way to her dad's office. She'd wanted to go as soon as Adam had left, but her dad had been busy assembling a team to work on The Mansion proposal. Then later on, she'd been caught up with HR, looking for a new head chef for one of their franchise owners.

Despite her attempts to settle her nerves, she couldn't contain her excitement as she approached his door. Her proposal for the Yosemite hotel was the only one he'd ever inquired about. That had to mean he was interested, right?

Paula, her dad's secretary, had already left for the day, so Olivia went straight towards his open door and knocked.

"Hello, sweetie," Dad said as she walked in. "How did everything go with The Granger?" he asked, referring to the Boston hotel she'd visited. "Were you able to talk to Peters?"

Larry Peters, the owner of the hotel, was supposed to

have contacted her last month about getting their much-needed renovation plans approved. But after the deadline had come and gone and her phone calls to him were left unanswered, she'd flown to Boston to see if there'd been any changes made to the hotel as well as to talk with him in person. Since he'd been avoiding her, she'd bypassed visiting his house and had instead cornered him at the race-track, where he'd had a horse running in the derby.

"Yes," she said as she sat in one of the chairs across her dad's desk. "He said that he was working with an architect on the plans, but after I asked to see what they've come up with, he admitted they were still searching for an architectural firm."

She doubted Peters would actually go through with the renovation. If he were serious, he could've asked her or someone else at Montgomery for a recommendation months ago when he'd first gotten their recommended improvement plan.

She hesitated before adding, "I think Peters is buying time while he looks for another hotel chain that's less demanding." For all she knew, he could already be negotiating a contract with someone else. He hadn't been particularly interested in what she'd had to say.

"I wouldn't be surprised. He's never been shy in complaining about our high standards."

While it was true that Montgomery's standards were higher than most, those standards had garnered them a loyal client base. The hotel owners who chose Montgomery Hotels were often lured by that built-in client base, but not every owner was prepared to invest in the upkeep required to achieve and maintain their high standards. She hated the thought of losing another one of their hotels, but it was better to do so than to have unsatisfied customers.

Since no final decision had been made in that regard, she continued, "They've fixed a few minor items on the improvement plan, including upgrading the lights." She held back on commenting that they'd probably only done so to lower their electricity bill. "I emailed you my report in addition to Jim's old one, but I think the most pressing issue is the guest bathrooms, which need a complete overhaul." She'd been disheartened by how worn everything had looked. There'd even been cracks in some of the sinks she'd looked at. "The service was good, but at times, they were understaffed. I spoke with the general manager about it and he said that there was a flu going around that caused the absences." But the fact that Jim, their renovations specialist, had also noted that they'd been understaffed during his review three months ago made the story less believable. And since the owner didn't care enough about the hotel to properly maintain it, it wasn't too far-fetched to think that he wasn't willing to keep a full staff either.

All the upgrades and staffing problems wouldn't be a problem if Montgomery owned the hotel. But this was one of their franchisees. Though all the improvements were for the good of the hotel, there were times the owners thought that they were unnecessary or just too expensive. What's worse was all the time she and Jim had spent trying to make the renovations more palatable to Peters.

She'd known Peters wouldn't be happy when he got the plan, so they'd stopped short of a full-on renovation that would've required the temporary closure of the hotel and had even broken down the improvement plan into two phases—the first dealing with things that needed to be fixed right away and the second dealing with improvements that would enhance the customers' experience.

And in return, they'd gotten crickets. It was frustrating, to say the least, but she kept her emotions in check. Her feelings wouldn't alter the situation one bit and her dad preferred to deal in facts.

"Let me know if you have any questions after reading the report." She was curious as to what her dad would do. In similar situations, she'd seen him do everything from offering to buy the hotel to dropping the property, and while it was rare for him to drop a hotel from their portfolio, she could definitely see it happening here. Peters had really shown his unprofessionalism by ignoring their calls and emails. "But in the meantime, I want to follow up on my Yosemite proposal."

"Ah, yes," Dad said as he leaned back against his chair. "A luxury hotel for the outdoor adventurer."

She actually had a plan for a small line of hotels near national parks and other outdoor attractions. The accommodation choices around national parks were often limited and if you wanted a five-star hotel? Forget about it.

Sure, there were a few and some were even inside the parks themselves, but they were often booked more than a year in advance. It was an underserved market and she thought Montgomery well-positioned to fill the void. It would also be a great way to introduce their brand to people who wouldn't have otherwise considered one of their hotels.

But they'd have to be selective about their locations. Business clients made up a large portion of Montgomery's repeat clientele, and most of the locations she was considering for this particular line were far away from any corporate headquarters. They'd have to rely on vacationers.

"You must admit we could've used a hotel like it once or twice," she said. Due to her dad's busy schedule, they rarely planned family vacations in advance. By the time they were ready to make a reservation, the hotels were often fully booked.

It didn't help that Dad was a stickler for never staying at a competitor's hotel, and he viewed almost everyone as a competitor, which vastly narrowed their choices. Outside of Montgomery properties, he was generally only willing to stay in independently owned hotels that weren't affiliated with any chains.

Whenever the hotels were fully booked, which was almost always, they usually ended up renting a house or a cabin. While Dad could've easily pulled a favor or paid someone to get a room, he wasn't like that. Being a hotelier who always put the customer first, he thought of reservations as sacred—even when it wasn't at his hotel.

"You think you're up for something this big?" he asked.

"I do." Not only was she excited to prove that she was capable of handling big projects like this, she wanted out of being a relations manager. He'd assigned her the position when she'd first joined Montgomery, saying that it was the best way to learn about the corporate side of the business. And while it was true that she'd learned a lot during her four years in the role, she wanted to do more.

Dad seemed to think about it for a second before nodding. "Good. Then I want you to take charge of The Mansion project." He waved his hand about. "I expect you've heard about the soon-to-be owner of The Mansion approaching us?"

"Yeah. I met Adam at the elevator this morning. Wait—does that mean we got it?"

Excitement coursed through her at the thought of getting her grandfather's hotel back into the family fold before she remembered how much Adam wanted to change it. He'd said he wanted to gut it. She couldn't do that to her grandfather's hotel. How could her dad even expect that of her? He knew how she felt about The Mansion.

"Well. Not yet. The team is still putting together a proposal, but I expect we'll be taking a fifty percent stake in the hotel. When the deal goes through, I want you to head the project." He leveled a stare at her. "I know how much you want to get The Mansion back for Grandpa, but I want no more of this crazy talk about restoring the hotel to its 'original glory.' It's ostentatious, gaudy, and out of date. You'd know it, too, if you took a real clear look at it."

Her back straightened. She'd never heard Dad talk about the hotel that way and her excitement took another hit. She'd wanted to get The Mansion back for their family for so long, but not this way. She couldn't destroy what her grandfather had built.

"If it's so bad, why do you want it?"

Besides the rooms, which even she admitted were dated and a little showy, the common areas of the hotel needed nothing more than a light restoration to bring out the beauty that was already there—not the gut job or whatever it was Adam had in mind. A chill ran down her back at the thought of The Mansion without its gorgeous ballroom and its beautiful tearoom. No. She couldn't let that happen.

Dad laughed. "Because I want it, too. It was your grandfather's first hotel—the one we built the Montgomery brand on. Can you imagine what a feat it would be to get it back?"

She blinked in surprise. After he'd rejected her proposal, she'd thought him uninterested in reacquiring the hotel. Instead, it had been her vision he hadn't liked, which didn't bode well for her plans to push for a restoration architect. Still, she intended to finish compiling her short list of possible firms to contact once the deal was done. Giving Adam options and ideas to save The Mansion's features just might be the key to stopping his plans to gut the hotel.

"Are you sure you're okay being partners with Adam?" she asked. Since they'd lost their previous Manhattan hotel due to unscrupulous business partners, she couldn't imagine her father wanting to jump into another partnership—especially one in New York. If things turned out badly again, the hotel would be a constant reminder of the bad partnership whenever they drove by it.

"He's adamant about retaining at least a portion of the ownership." Dad shrugged. "Besides, he seems like a decent enough fellow."

It took every effort not to roll her eyes. As always, Dad

was more of a people person, preferring to base his decisions on his intuition and gut impressions of a person's character while leaving others to deal with the mechanics of the deal. Though it seemed like a crazy way to do business, he'd done very well with it.

"But what about my proposal?" She'd thought it as good as done.

"Why don't we see how things go with The Mansion and revisit your proposal at the beginning of the year?"

Disappointment bit at her even though she knew it was a more than reasonable proposition. Sure, she'd worked on renovations before, but she'd never been solely in charge of a project of this magnitude before—everything from the renovation to the transition of management and operations. In fact, taking charge of The Mansion project would be a step up for her. It wouldn't be as big a step up as her Yosemite project would've been, but it was one nonetheless.

Still, because he hadn't immediately rejected her Yosemite proposal, she'd taken it as a sign that he would accept it. She'd built her hopes up and had already been thinking about what would come afterwards. To be relegated into doing another renovation for one of their franchisees—even if it was for her grandfather's hotel—felt like she was taking a step back.

"What would you have done if Adam hadn't approached us?" she couldn't help but ask.

"I would've put you in charge of a different hotel." Dad shrugged. "I was actually thinking about offering to buy The Granger from Peters if he continues to put up a fight about renovations. I still might."

She should be thrilled that he was giving her the chance to prove herself with such a big undertaking. Instead, she couldn't help but think that the reason he was putting her through such a test was because of what happened with the Whitcombe, their previous Manhattan hotel.

About a year after she'd joined Montgomery, their partner in the Whitcombe had begun complaining about their high operating costs and had wanted to change operators. At the time, Montgomery had had a list of approved operators to manage Montgomery-branded hotels, so she'd allowed the change without consulting her father. It hadn't seemed worth the time and effort to fight with Gen Capital about the costs and she'd naively thought they'd come back once they saw that Montgomery's expenditures were justified.

But barely a year later, their internal auditor discovered that Gen Capital had colluded with the operator to fix the books and make their profits seem lower than they actually were while pocketing the difference.

Dad sold their remaining stake in the hotel to Gen Capital after he'd found out. Since stress was what had most likely caused his heart attack, he and Mom decided that it wasn't worth it to fight to recoup the losses and the embezzled profits.

And though Montgomery had made money, the outcome had hurt—not only because they'd sold their stake for less than it was worth, but because they'd put so much into the property. Hell, Olivia and her brother had practically grown up in the Whitcombe. They'd spent almost every day after school there doing just about every chore imaginable. And though she more often than not had hated her chores, it had seemed inconceivable for the hotel not to be a part of the Montgomery family.

Olivia knew her dad's decision to sell had more to do about his lack of confidence in her ability than wanting to avoid stress. He simply hadn't trusted her to get the job done. She had no doubt Dad would've chosen to fight if his longtime trusted advisor, Gene Cunningham, hadn't retired and had still been at the company. Dad had always been the take-no-prisoners kind of guy when it came to business, which was how he'd grown Montgomery in such a short time.

But not only had he chosen not to fight, he'd also completely stopped licensing their brand to new hotels if they didn't also manage them. It was the surest way to control quality, he'd said.

Dad had told her that she'd made the right call, but she wasn't convinced and had been trying to make up for her mistake ever since.

"All right," she said cautiously. She'd do well on this assignment and prove she was capable of executing her Yosemite plan. Furthermore, as manager of The Mansion project, she'd be in charge of the renovations and would be in a better position to preserve her grandfather's legacy as best as she could.

"So, what do you think about Adam?" her dad asked.

Her cheeks flushed as she remembered Adam's smile. It seemed it wasn't only Carol who was a sucker for a handsome face. As much as Olivia hated that he wanted to change her grandfather's hotel so drastically, she couldn't deny that there was something undeniably sexy about him. And the fact that he'd chosen to become a land developer instead of just relying on his family's money spoke highly of his character.

"He seems like a decent enough guy. I didn't get a chance to really talk with him."

"I think he's single," Dad said, and she groaned.

"Dad, you know I'm not interested in seeing anyone right now." She barely had any free time as it was. When she wasn't managing crises, she was working on getting her proposals off the ground. Her dad would eventually approve one of them and when he did, she didn't want any distractions, romantic or otherwise. She couldn't afford any.

It was insane. Her dad had never approved of any of her boyfriends. It was like he'd believed no man could ever be good enough for his only daughter. But now that she was older, he was practically throwing every single man at her. He sometimes even asked her about William Yates, whom she'd dated in high school and college. Dad hadn't hidden his displeasure when she and William were together, but now that they'd broken up, Dad often acted as if William was the son-in-law who could've been.

"Well, I was hoping that you'd changed your mind. How about Mark Callahan's son? He's recently come back from Singapore."

"Dad!"

"I know. I know," he said as he raised his palms. "No personal talk in the office. But be warned, your mother and I won't let up on this."

Smiling, she shook her head as she stood. Her parents

were incorrigible, especially when it came to the idea of her settling down. They really wanted grandchildren. And while she wanted children someday, too, she wanted to build a career to be proud of first. Oftentimes, she felt as if she were just leaching off her parents' goodwill.

"I think you'll have better luck with Robbie," she said, and Dad snorted. Her brother was a proud bachelor, but since he was three years older than her, she figured he should be the one saddled with the responsibility of giving their parents grandchildren. "And thank you for the opportunity." It wasn't what she wanted, but she understood she needed to prove herself first.

"Don't let me down, sugar," he said as she reached the door.

"I won't."

* * *

Adam's cell phone rang as he walked into his apartment later that week. He checked the screen and saw Jake Halliday's name. They'd closed the sale on The Mansion yesterday, so Adam figured the hedge fund manager was calling to say something along the lines of "It was great doing business with you."

"Good evening, Jake. Do you have another hotel to offer me?" Adam joked as he set his briefcase on the coffee table. He'd met Jake at a party last year and had been surprised when the man had called asking if Adam was interested in purchasing The Mansion. The hotel had been used to pay off part of a debt and Jake had needed quick liquidity.

At the time, Adam had already been entertaining thoughts of entering the New York market in some way, but the high property prices had always stopped him. Though New York real estate prices rose at a much higher pace than in Texas, it was still hard to stomach.

Four hundred million in New York was nothing compared to what four hundred million could buy in Texas. But he recognized a good deal when he saw one, and The Mansion was definitely that.

"Ha. No. I just wanted to let you know that there've been some whispers circulating about you being financially insolvent."

Adam frowned. "You know that's not true." If it were, he wouldn't have been able to get a loan to finance the hotel purchase and they wouldn't have been able to close the deal as quickly as they had.

"I know—I did my own research. But I thought you should know what's being said."

"Did you hear anything else?"

There was a pause before Jake answered, "Just that your developments in Texas aren't doing so well. A lot of vacancies, delays... That sort of thing."

That wasn't true, either, and could easily be checked by visiting any of his developments. Instinctively, he knew where these rumors were coming from: his parents. They were always saying bad things about him, making him out to be the black sheep of the family, but this was the first time he'd heard about them trying to ruin a business deal of his.

Part of him couldn't believe they'd stoop so low, but he

should've expected it. After years of them belittling him to anyone who would listen, his continued success was bound to look bad on them and their decision to cut him off. But instead of admitting their mistakes, they'd chosen to continue dirtying his name. He didn't know why he was surprised. He, of all people, knew what they were capable of.

"All right. Thanks for letting me know." He didn't know Jake that well, but he certainly wouldn't mind getting to know the guy better. Judging by their dealings on The Mansion and from this call, Jake was a straight shooter, which was a pleasant surprise. There weren't a lot of people like him in the business world.

"Of course. How's it going with The Mansion?"

Adam sighed. "I'm still working it out with an operator." The negotiations with Montgomery Hotels weren't going as quickly as he'd hoped. Victor had, once again, offered to buy the whole hotel from him.

Victor had offered a fair price, one that would've given Adam a tidy profit, but as Adam had already stated, he wasn't interested. He wanted to see this project through and now that his parents knew about it, he wanted the property and its prestige even more. He'd make them eat their words and regret what they'd done to him. And the way to do that was through The Mansion.

Adam had finally reached a tentative agreement with Montgomery yesterday. They were still working on all the details and terms, but he expected it to be finalized soon.

"How's everything on your end?" he asked Jake. With all the due diligence and inspections required to close The

Mansion deal, these past few weeks had been incredibly hectic for Adam. Given that Jake was navigating the sale of multiple properties and companies in this deal with Quinley, Adam couldn't even begin to imagine Jake's workload.

Jake laughed. "I wish everyone was as easy to deal with as you are. I now own Gerard, because a buyer fell through."

"I'm sure you'll find another buyer for it." Gerard was a well-known chocolate chain with shops all over the world. In fact, his sister was one of their biggest fans. He couldn't imagine Jake having a hard time finding a buyer for it.

"You wouldn't happen to be interested in it, too, now would you?"

Adam laughed. "Thanks for thinking of me, but I need to focus on The Mansion right now." Especially now that his parents knew about it, he couldn't let it fail. He couldn't afford to.

"It was worth a shot. Let me know if you change your mind."

After they made plans to meet for lunch when things settled down, Adam hung up and turned his attention to those rumors. His parents had to be the source.

Sure, he wasn't particularly known for his kindness in his business dealings. But he'd never screwed anyone over. He always made sure his deals were fair to all parties involved or he didn't do them. The only people who had a gripe with him were, frankly, his parents. They'd expected him to crawl back home after blowing through his trust fund. Instead, he'd grown that trust fund into a small empire.

Spreading rumors about him was probably their way of getting him to reach out to them, so that he would, once again, dance to their tune. But he refused to give them the satisfaction. He'd be a success in his own right and let them stew in that!

## CHAPTER THREE

"She really is a beauty, isn't she?" Ricky Devine said as he and Adam approached The Mansion.

"She is," Adam said, agreeing with his second in command. The historic hotel was a sight to behold and held its own amongst the breathtaking skyline of Manhattan. Though not as tall as some of the neighboring structures, its design and workmanship cemented its position as one of the most striking buildings in town. And it only got better on closer inspection. During the daytime, such as now, one could really see all the details that had been put into it— Gothic parapets, patterned brickwork, intricate bronze window frames…

The building was in a completely separate class from the hotels he'd developed in the past and a testament to how far he'd come in his career. He'd gone from developing a small strip mall with a mere five stores to this.

It was still crazy to think of sometimes. After he'd

broken free of his parents' grasp, he'd searched for a way to make money so that he wouldn't have to rely on anyone ever again. And now, he was on his way to creating an empire that would soon match theirs. The fact that he'd built his from scratch—rather than inheriting it—was infinitely more satisfying.

The doorman opened the door for them, and they stepped into the warm foyer. As always, the ostentatious decor struck a discordant note for him. Even after all his visits to The Mansion, experiencing the flashy, overblown interior after appreciating the understated beauty of the exterior was jarring. He couldn't wait to get the redesign underway to clear away the eyesore.

Scanning the reception area, his gaze zeroed in on Olivia, who was wearing a light green dress that showed off her toned legs. Remembering that she was a business part-ner, he forced his gaze upwards and saw that she was talking to a tall blonde woman near the front desk. He started towards them and Olivia's gaze rose to meet his, a smile curving her beautiful lips.

"Thanks for coming," she said as she met him halfway, then firmly shook his hand.

"Of course." She'd already sent him a long list of improvements the hotel needed, but she'd also wanted to do a walk-through to ensure they were on the same page before reaching out to architectural firms for proposals.

He'd be the first to admit that he hadn't been particu-larly thrilled when Olivia had been assigned as The Mansion's project manager. Though he'd enjoyed talking with her when they'd first met, he'd suspected her father had given her the job out of nepotism. And his online searches on her had only cemented his worries. There'd been absolutely nothing about her professional qualifications or achievements with Montgomery or any of their business dealings. All that had appeared were pictures of her at charity events and parties. He'd been prepared to ask Victor to replace Olivia with someone more capable of managing the project, but after a few email exchanges with her, he realized that he had nothing to worry about. This wasn't a token job for her. She knew what she was doing, and she worked quickly.

"This is Ricky Devine," he said, performing the introductions.

Olivia beamed as she shook Ricky's hand. "Hi, Ricky. It's good to finally put a face to the name."

Irritation coursed through Adam at how animated she'd suddenly become. Why hadn't she acted the same way towards him? He belatedly remembered that the two must have exchanged a few emails regarding The Mansion since he'd put Ricky in charge of the project on his end. It was probably only natural to be excited to finally meet the person she'd be working closely with during the renovations.

The thought of the two working together troubled him, and he froze. Where was this sudden jealousy coming from? Sure, he would've asked her out if he'd met her at a party, but they were business partners, so that was a no-go. He knew better than to mix business with pleasure and was pretty sure Ricky wouldn't, either.

So why, then, did he want to tell Ricky to let go of her

hand? His lack of sleep must finally be getting to him and he silently vowed to delegate more of his workload to others.

"It's good to meet you as well," Ricky said, then finally released her hand.

Olivia then introduced Natalie McCombs, who was the standards specialist for Montgomery. After he and Ricky shook hands with Natalie, Olivia nodded at them. "Do you want to start from the bottom then go up?"

"Sure," he said.

"Did you get a chance to look at the portfolios of the two architectural firms I sent over?" she asked as they made their way towards the elevator.

"Yeah. I like Axe more, but I'm good with either." Both firms had done some wonderful work modernizing historic buildings.

"Great," she said as they stepped into an open elevator. "We already have all the existing as-built drawings and the various engineering reports ready, so we just need to add what we talk about today before reaching out to them."

The elevator closed and he realized she was wearing perfume. It was a light floral scent that smelled deliciously sweet. Or perhaps it was her shampoo? He resisted the urge to lean over and find out.

"How about the list of improvements? Was there anything you wanted to add to it?" she asked, and he had to force himself to remember what they were talking about.

"I was wondering why you wanted to move the gym." She wanted to move it from the basement to one of the top floors, which seemed completely unnecessary, especially when doing so would make it smaller. Sure, the space could use a facelift and new machines, but the current location was fine where it was.

"I want to give our customers another view besides the television or the mirrors while they work out. I admit we won't have as much space upstairs, but two thousand square feet should be more than enough for a hotel our size. Besides, we could use the current gym area to expand the spa as well as to provide a bigger computer room for all the new servers we'll be putting in." The elevator doors opened, and she stepped out. "The existing computer room is a little too small and gets too hot for our comfort, but we can make up for the extra room with the office space we're freeing up."

And Adam knew they were upgrading the systems for everything from the conference rooms to the elevators.

"You mentioned a software that would automate the back-office processes in your email," Ricky said. "Can you expand more on that?"

Olivia nodded and began talking about how their proprietary accounting software had an integrated customer management module that allowed it to do every-thing from reconciling their bookkeeping to assigning guest rooms based on the customer's preferences.

It was a more robust system than what Adam used in his hotels, but more importantly, Montgomery wasn't using it as a means of reducing customer interaction. And he real-ized it wasn't just the design and amenities that set a Mont-gomery hotel apart from the others; it was the customer service as well. Hell, even Montgomery's willingness to take the time to go through each of the rooms, making sure everyone was in agreement, showed just how much they cared about his opinion and satisfaction. Perhaps it was because he'd been building hotels from the ground up, but Stone House, the operator for his other hotels, had never once done that. They'd just given him the specifications and set him up with the right people.

Seeing how willing Montgomery was to go the extra distance, he knew he'd made the correct decision by partnering with them. They'd do right by The Mansion.

* * *

"And replace the gold railings with a glass one," Adam said as he glanced at the leveled stories of the atrium.

Olivia inwardly groaned as Ricky diligently added the item to Adam's ever-growing list of demands. This walkthrough wasn't going anywhere near as planned.

She'd foolishly thought walking Adam through each of the rooms would make him appreciate The Mansion's beauty and unique charm, so he'd rethink his plans for a full-scale renovation. Instead, he seemed to be taking great delight in imagining all the different ways they could modernize the hotel.

Thinking of Adam's request, Olivia glanced at the gold railings. She loved the delicate flower designs and thought they offered a whimsical, lighthearted element that complemented the somber marble flooring. If it were up to her, she'd keep the railings and work the rest of the design around them.

*It's ostentatious, gaudy, and out of date.*

Her father's words echoed in her ear, causing her to wonder if she was, in fact, clinging to an idealized memory.

Keeping an open mind, she looked up and imagined how a glass railing would look—first as someone looking up from the main lobby floor, then as someone looking down from one of the upper floors. She then tried to picture how the various parts might flow together.

"I'm not sure if glass will work with the current design," she finally admitted. While it would suit the stained-glass ceiling more than the existing metal railings did, the individual components just didn't mesh as a whole. "But I think it could definitely work if we revamped the whole atrium with updated lights, new floors, a different color palette… The scheme wouldn't complement the tearoom, but it would segue well into the shops."

"I don't think we need to factor in the tearoom's current design," Adam said as he walked towards the space, stopping on the threshold to glance around the room. "I'm thinking it'll look better with leather chairs, wood-paneled walls, that sort of thing."

*No, not the tearoom.*

Sure, the majority of tearooms were decorated in a similar vein, but the business-like atmosphere of those spaces always reminded her more of a corporate boardroom than an elegant restaurant in which to have a light meal.

She could still remember the first time her grandparents had taken her for tea when she was seven. She'd been awestruck by the chandeliers and the stained-glass windows, the fancy linens, and the pretty dishes. The Mansion had seemed like a fairytale castle and the tearoom a princess's room. Her grandparents had even dressed her up as a princess for the visit.

It hadn't mattered to Grandpa that he didn't own The Mansion anymore and that his company owned a competing hotel the next block over. In his mind, it would always be his since he'd not only created the hotel, but had practically grown up in the building when it housed their bank.

Unfortunately, Dad had found out about the visits after the second one and had forbidden any more. Unless they were attending a party or were contemplating managing or buying the hotel, Dad was against any family members being seen in one of their competitors' hotels. One never knew when you could be photographed, and he didn't want to give anyone the ammunition to hurt their business.

She hadn't really understood what was happening at the time and had been devastated when she'd found out that she couldn't go to the beautiful castle again. To make it up to her, Grandpa had had a dollhouse based on The Mansion made for her. It had the lobby with its high ceiling, the ballroom with its beautiful arches and columns, and a few guestrooms where she'd loved to tuck her dolls in at night.

"Is there anything about the room you'd like to keep?" she asked, resisting the urge to point out how generic the tearoom would look if they implemented his suggestions. Why have a version of what everyone else had when they could have this unique space? How did he not appreciate the castle-like feel of the room?

He shook his head. "No. I don't think we need to save anything. I'm thinking clear windows, raised panel ceilings, and low hanging lights."

She forced a smile. "I'll include those in my notes, but perhaps it would be best to keep the design brief on a broad level for now. We want to encourage the architects to bring their best ideas forward rather than to dictate restraints at this stage." She wasn't sure how much more of this she could take. He was crushing her dreams with every word out of his mouth.

Adam laughed. "Of course. I understand the need for creative freedom."

She sincerely doubted he knew what creative freedom was. The way he'd been pointing out changes to every single space—changes that would reduce The Mansion to a cookie-cutter replica of every other hotel—suggested he had no creative impulses at all!

She inwardly sighed as she stopped herself. She wasn't being fair to him. Sure, his vision for the hotel was different from hers but that didn't mean he was without creativity. Although how he could see the stained-glass windows and the painted ceiling and want to get rid of them was beyond her. There was no way an architect in his or her right mind would even suggest that.

She froze at the thought and realized that she'd been worrying for nothing. Sure, Adam wanted to change a lot of things, but he wasn't trained in architecture or design. He was just pointing out what he didn't like and suggesting "fixes." The architect, on the other hand, would look at the building's design as a whole.

And from her experience working with Axe, she was positive they'd come up with a solution that not only Adam would approve of, but would also keep the spirit of her grandfather's hotel alive. Relief swamped her and she continued the tour with a lightened heart.

# CHAPTER FOUR

"I sure hope we'll be able to lease one of your spaces," Emilia Cruz said over the phone and Olivia beamed. It felt good to have people excited about The Mansion.

Since news of the acquisition spread, quite a few fashion houses had reached out to them about renting their retail spaces. The Mansion's Upper Fifth Avenue real estate was already highly coveted, but Montgomery's new management made it even more so.

"I'll contact you in a month or so when we know more." Her dad was looking at bigger, more established names than Emilia Cruz's eponymous brand, but Emilia was quickly becoming the go-to designer for evening gowns. Olivia would love to be ahead of the curve on this one by giving Emilia retail space at The Mansion, but knew the decision also depended on the other tenants they got.

"Thanks! I appreciate it."

Pride filled Olivia as she hung up a few minutes later. The fact that so many people were interested in doing business with The Mansion without even seeing their renovation plans was a testament to the strength of Montgomery's brand. And sure, the family bank had made them a household name before they'd ever opened a hotel, but it was her father's and grandfather's hard work that had made Montgomery Hotels the brand it was today. While she wasn't always happy with her job, she loved the idea of continuing the family legacy.

Thinking of the family legacy, she remembered that she was still waiting to hear back from the architect. She checked her email and saw that Seth Tanner had finally sent his concept designs for The Mansion. Eager to see what he'd come up with, she opened the attachment.

She scanned the section where he detailed the touch-ups he recommended for the exterior, then scrolled down to the interior renderings. She frowned when she saw the sleek, modern design of the new lobby. Without its signature Roman columns and chandeliers, the space was unrecognizable as the same hotel and she couldn't help but wonder if there'd been a mix up with another project. She glanced at the next image—a perspective of the ballroom—and frowned when she saw the Venetian windows. They were the same ones The Mansion had, which meant there hadn't been a mistake.

Aghast, she looked back at the first picture and tried to superimpose the design on the current layout in her head. She was honest enough to admit that she would've liked the design if it were for a new hotel, but not for The Mansion. This minimalist approach was all wrong for her grandfather's glamorous hotel and stripped away its character and spirit. The low hanging lights and subtle play of tone-on-tone colors made it look like thousands of other hotels and she doubted anyone would prefer the wide-open spaces to the lush seating area they currently had.

She couldn't believe it. When Seth had renovated their Charleston hotel, he'd barely touched the place. He'd designed these small modifications that had made the world of difference, blending the traditional with enough modern sensibility to be delightfully refreshing. She'd been expecting something similar with The Mansion—which was one of the reasons she'd wanted him to work on the project—but these designs were like they'd been created by a completely different person.

Perhaps she should've told Seth that she was only looking for small changes, but on top of not wanting to directly counter her father's and Adam's wishes, she hadn't wanted to stifle or dictate the architect's creativity.

Besides, she'd thought he'd see what she saw: a beautiful, traditional hotel that had been neglected. She'd never imagined he would suggest such radical changes. He'd proposed a bold design that visibly introduced a modern, minimalist aesthetic that played off a few carefully selected elements of the historic building. A bold look into the future with a respectful nod to glimpses of the past, she supposed if she were to be whimsical about his renderings. She respected Seth's vision and admired so much of his work, so... Was it possible her dad and Adam were right about The Mansion needing more than a minor facelift?

Seth wouldn't have recommended these changes if he didn't think it was for the betterment of the hotel. She thought about The Mansion's elegant lobby with its Old World charm, remembered that feeling of stepping into a fantasy world when she was a child experiencing her first high tea, and inwardly cursed herself for even considering the betraying thought. No. The lobby was perfect just the way it was. Seth simply hadn't connected with it.

She'd contact the other architectural firm she'd shortlisted and pay the fees for another set of concept designs out of her own pocket. Then she'd give Adam the choice between the two. In the meantime, she'd tell Adam's team that she hadn't gotten Axe's designs yet.

They were expecting to see the proposals today and had even pushed back their weekly meeting from Wednesday to today because of it. But she couldn't risk Adam seeing these designs. Instinctively, she knew that they were just what he was looking for and that he'd approve them without hesitation. But she couldn't let that happen. She needed to give him an option that retained more of The Mansion's charm while updating the overall feel of the building so that he could make an informed decision. If he still chose Seth's design…well, then at least she'd know she'd tried her best.

She sighed as she pulled up her notes to review for today's status meeting. She'd call the other architectural firm this afternoon—after the meeting. Hopefully, they could rush a design of at least the lobby, if not all the public rooms.

Once she was done reviewing her notes, she left her office and headed towards the meeting room. She had just passed the break station when she heard a familiar male voice. "Hello, again."

She turned and saw Adam approaching her. He didn't usually attend these weekly meetings and she felt a twinge of guilt at the realization that he'd probably made an exception because he wanted to see Axe's designs.

"Hi."

"Have you heard from the architect yet?" he asked, confirming her guess.

"No. I just got an email saying that they're delayed," she said and immediately felt bad about lying. But the stakes were too high. She couldn't let her grandfather's hotel be destroyed. "I'll let you know as soon as I get them," she added to soften the blow, but it didn't make her feel any better.

While her grandfather might have approved of her lying —after all, he'd been known to be a ruthless businessman— her dad certainly wouldn't. Her parents had always taught her to be straight and honest, and she hated the thought of letting them down even if they didn't know about what she'd done. They'd taught her better than that.

"Thanks. I hope the wait will be worth it," Adam said, and Olivia suddenly grasped how bad her lie would reflect on Seth.

Sure, Seth *had* sent the designs a few hours late, but it wouldn't be anything like the weeks she'd make the delay out to be as she waited on the other architect.

"So, how have things been going with you?" Adam asked as they started towards the meeting room.

"I'm doing all right. How about you?"

He sighed. "Busy. The hard rain is causing delays for our Houston project. Everyone is trying to work around it so that we can open in time. Ricky was supposed to come to the meeting today, but he hasn't gotten back yet."

"Another complex?" From what she understood, shopping complexes, as opposed to hotels, seemed to be his forte.

"Don't sound too impressed," he said, and she couldn't help but smile when she saw the laughter in his brown eyes. She couldn't deny that he was charming and her attraction to him somehow worsened the fact that he was trying to ruin her lifelong dream. "But yeah, another shopping complex." They reached the meeting room, and he opened the door for her.

"Thanks," she murmured as she walked in. It was still early, but everyone had already gathered. The room suddenly became quiet, and it took her a second to realize that everyone was waiting for her to take charge. The reminder that it was *her* project was a sobering yet exciting thought. If this project was successful, she could very well be launching her own sub-brand of hotels next year.

Adam sat and she began talking about how Montgomery had reached an agreement with The Mansion's current operator, Prism, to manage the hotel until they closed for renovations. Since they'd be closing the hotel soon, it didn't make sense to retrain all the employees to conform with Montgomery's standards or to switch to their computer system.

But as everyone presented their updates, she couldn't stop thinking about the concept designs she'd gotten and knew she'd only given herself a temporary reprieve. Just because she intended to engage another architect didn't mean Adam would approve of their designs, but she had to try. She'd never forgive herself if she didn't.

* * *

Olivia sighed as she stepped into The Mansion's gilded lobby that night. Guilt over her duplicity had wracked her all day and she knew she wouldn't be able to hold out until the other architect sent their designs.

Why she'd thought she could sustain the lie for weeks, she didn't know. She hadn't even been able to handle the guilt that one time she'd had a half-day at school and hadn't told her parents. Thinking that she'd get assigned extra duties at the hotel, she'd chosen to go shopping with her friends instead. She'd ended up feeling horrible and had confessed to her dad as soon as she got to the hotel later that day.

She couldn't even handle a lie by omission where no one got hurt, and yet she'd thought she could pull off a full-on lie that would make someone she respected and considered a friend look bad? Yeah, right. She'd come clean to Adam tomorrow, then step down from the project. She'd be kissing away her dreams of a Yosemite hotel, but considering how she was acting, she didn't deserve it.

She'd failed her grandpa again.

Worse, this time she'd let her parents down as well. She'd assured her father that she'd handle the project with an open mind. Not only had she not done that, but she'd also lied about receiving the architect's designs. She'd been so blinded by the desire to revive her grandfather's hotel that she hadn't considered who she'd hurt or the damage she'd cause.

But she hadn't known what to do. When Adam had asked about the designs, her only thought had been a panicked notion that he couldn't see them. The images were too similar to his ideas and she'd known, beyond doubt, that he would approve of them.

She shoved her hands into her pockets and took a long look around the lobby that her grandfather had spent so much time creating. A part of her felt relieved that she was coming clean, but at the same time, her heart felt as if it were breaking in two.

Her grandfather had put so much of himself into The Mansion. He'd designed the whimsical gilt railings based on her grandmother's favorite flower and had even gone to Murano to commission the chandeliers by the famous glass-makers. And now, it would all be replaced with something modern and edgy, without heart or unique character. Not that she had a problem with being modern or edgy, but she hated the thought of it here, in place of her grandfather's design. Minimalism had no place in The Mansion.

But that was what both Adam and her dad wanted, and she had to remember that.

It wouldn't make a difference if she *could* handle the guilt until the new architect's designs came in, because what she wanted simply wasn't the vision they were looking for. She sighed as she sat on one of the couches. It was hard to believe that in two years' time, this would all be gone.

She guessed she'd always thought The Mansion of her

grandfather's pictures would live on forever. Sure, there'd been additions—like the gym and the spa—and some changes, such as the bar moving next to the main restaurant, but the basic design had always remained intact regardless of the ownership.

It devastated her to think that they, her grandfather's own family, would be the ones to change the hotel so drastically, that they would be the ones to put his dreams and ideas to death. It was such a betrayal.

But that's how things were in the cutthroat hospitality industry—hotels were constantly adapting to keep up with the changes in customers' tastes and demands.

Her cell phone rang in her bag. She didn't feel like answering, but when she saw that it was Stacy Lang, she stood and went to an unoccupied meeting room to answer. She always took calls from family, and her best friend since preschool was definitely that.

"Hey, Stacy," she said as she closed the door.

"Hey, Livie, where are you right now?"

"I'm at The Mansion."

"Are you serious? You're still working?"

"No. I've just been doing some thinking." She hesitated before adding, "I've decided to step down from the project."

"What? Why? You've been talking about getting The Mansion back since we were kids!"

"That was before I had to clean any bathrooms," Olivia joked, then sighed at Stacy's silence. Though it was true that she hadn't wanted anything to do with the hospitality industry after she'd had to work at the Whitcombe every day after school, she'd grown to love working at Montgomery Hotels these past few years. "I don't want to be the one that destroys what my grandfather built." She then told Stacy about Seth's designs and how she'd pretended she hadn't received them. "If I can do something that underhanded now, how can I trust myself to make the right decisions in the future and not sabotage the project? I just can't keep an objective perspective, so the best thing for me to do is to step down."

"They really want to tear everything down?" Stacy asked. "Even the tearoom?"

"Yeah."

"But it's so gorgeous! How could they want to demolish it? Besides, it's always full. I'm pretty sure most of those customers aren't even staying at the hotel." There was a pause, then a snap of fingers. "I got it. Do you have the breakdown of the revenue for the tearoom?"

"I'm not sure." She had the food and beverage numbers as a whole but wasn't sure if they were separated into different restaurants or not. "But I can check."

"It might help to make a chart comparing the tearoom's revenue to the hotel's occupancy rate during the same period. That could show how much New Yorkers adore the restaurant—like it's a local treasure. Adam and your dad might not care for its beauty, but I'm sure the numbers will speak to them."

"Oh, my goodness. That's a great idea. Thank you!" Surely, Adam and her father wouldn't push for such a drastic renovation of the tearoom if the sales were strong enough in its current iteration. It seemed so simple. Why hadn't she thought of it?

A small voice in her head told her that it was because she was an impostor when it came to business and perhaps that was why her father continued to reject her proposals even though the underlying concepts were solid ideas. She'd never been interested in finance and revenue or budgets and marketing, and her father knew that. Hell, she wouldn't have even known how to do all those projections she'd included in her proposal if she hadn't asked for other people's help. It seemed no matter how many times financial reports were explained to her, she just didn't get it. Perhaps she should pick up a book or take some courses to learn more about business—that is, if Dad didn't immediately fire her after he found out about what she'd done.

In the meantime, she was so grateful Stacy had called and was sure her friend's intuition was right. She might not be able to save the lobby, but perhaps she could still save the tearoom and the ballroom. While not the leading venue it once was, The Mansion still drew in a respectable amount of business for parties and galas.

Stacy sighed. "I guess that means you won't be free for drinks tonight?"

"I'm sorry. Now that you've given me the idea, I want to run these numbers as soon as possible. Can I take a raincheck for tomorrow?"

"Okay, but I'm picking the place."

Knowing that Stacy was just making sure they didn't go to The Tavern again, Olivia couldn't help but smile. Unlike her, who always stayed with the tried and true, Stacy loved trying new restaurants and bars.

"All right. Just let me know where."

Olivia hung up and thought about what would happen if Stacy's intuition was correct. Would bringing solid revenue numbers to Adam's attention be enough to make up for what she'd done? To let her stay on the project?

Probably not. Though Adam was always cordial, Olivia was sure he was tough as nails when it came to business. After she came clean, she had no doubt he'd see her as the enemy. No. It was better to step down than to have him ask Dad to replace her.

But at least there was a chance the ballroom and tearoom could be saved. She smiled as she thought of the future visitors the tearoom would delight—of all the little girls who'd enjoy the castle-like atmosphere as she had. She should've called Stacy about her problem earlier, but she'd been so worried about Seth's designs that she simply hadn't been thinking.

If Stacy hadn't preempted her, Olivia would've most likely called her tomorrow—after her meeting with Adam, but by then it would've been too late. It was a huge stroke of luck that Stacy had called tonight, and Olivia breathed a sigh of thankfulness. Not only did Stacy always have the best ideas, she also had amazing timing.

* * *

Adam frowned as he read the proposal from a clothing store to lease one of the spaces in the Plex, the shopping complex he was building in Houston. An affordable yet trendy chain targeted towards teenagers, Wily Wear was quickly becoming a household name.

The owners knew it, too, and were trying to negotiate for a lower rent. The percentage of their store sales he'd get would definitely make up for the lower rent if their sales were strong, but that was a big if. Oftentimes, brands were hip for a few years then fell out of vogue when the next big thing hit.

Curious, he pulled up their website. The women's line of clothing seemed to be full of bright shirts and sundresses, while the men's section was full of T-shirts emblazoned with what he was sure were references to something—he just didn't know what.

Shaking his head, he closed the browser. He'd put out a feeler to his employees with teenagers to get their kids' opinions on the store. He usually asked his sister about these things but figured Martha wouldn't know anything about teens' clothing. The thought of his sister made him smile. It'd almost been a month since he'd last seen her and even longer since he'd seen their brother, Doug. Perhaps he'd invite them to dinner next week.

He was just about to call Martha when his intercom beeped.

"An Olivia Montgomery is here to see you," Caitlin, his receptionist, said.

His heart skipped a beat before reality set in. Just because he'd enjoyed talking with her yesterday didn't mean she was visiting him for personal reasons. It was more likely that she'd gotten the designs from the architect and had wanted to talk to him about them. Either way, he was happy to see her again. He quickly pressed the button on his phone. "Let her in. Thanks."

Olivia stepped into his office a few moments later, wearing a fitted white blouse and a black skirt. "I have Axe's designs," she said as she handed a folder to him.

She was here for work.

He shoved his disappointment aside. The design concepts must be really good for her to deliver them in person. He automatically flipped straight to the renderings. With the perfect mix of classiness and comfort, the designs were even better than what he'd expected. They were elegant and modern yet approachable and were absolutely perfect for bringing The Mansion forward into this century.

Before he could tell Olivia to hire the firm, she said, "I'm afraid I haven't been completely honest with you." She nodded at the proposal in his hand. "I actually got that yesterday afternoon—before the meeting. I didn't share it, because I didn't want to destroy what my grandfather made."

Surprised, he looked at her. He hadn't been expecting that.

Of course, he knew that The Mansion had been built by her grandfather, but he hadn't spared that fact another thought. Sentimentality didn't have a place in his world and, in his experience, the people who claimed to be motivated by it were just holding out for a better deal. But he had a niggling feeling Olivia was the real deal—and for that, he had no strategy.

"I'm taking myself out of the project," she continued,

then handed him another folder. "These were my plans for The Mansion. I haven't given them to anyone else on the project team, so you can use them as you will."

Curious, he took the folder and opened it. It was another business outline like the one she'd given him at the first meeting, but an expanded version. Once again, he was impressed by how detailed everything was. She had so many ideas—everything from engaging a local soap manufacturer for the room toiletries to adding extra meeting rooms on the top floor.

"You did all this?" he asked as he continued scanning the report.

"Let's just say that I've been thinking about this for a while." She hesitated before continuing, "And I hope you'll reconsider demolishing the tearoom and the ballroom. I've included the individual revenues for both spaces at the end and, as you can see, although the occupancy rates for the hotel have declined, the revenues for the ballroom stayed constant and the revenues of the tearoom actually increased during the same period." Intrigued, he looked at the chart and saw that she was right.

"I'll think about it." He'd have someone double-check the numbers. If this was really the case, then taking a lighter hand in renovating the rooms was a no-brainer. It would be cheaper, too.

"I'll have Donovan Riley take over as project manager for Montgomery," Olivia continued. "He's really good and doesn't have any of the personal hang-ups about the hotel that I do."

Adam sighed as he set the folder down. "You know, I

wouldn't be pushing for the changes if I didn't think they would make the hotel better. If I'm being honest, I think your grandfather's name was the only reason the hotel did so well when it opened."

If anyone else had built it, all the chandeliers, gold furnishings, and overdone decor would have been considered tacky and gauche. But because the Elliott Montgomery had built it, The Mansion had become a status symbol for those who had money and a glimpse inside how the other side lived for those who didn't. And it still was, he thought, if the numbers Olivia had given him were any indication. Of course, he'd always known the ballroom was a popular venue, but he'd always thought it was because of the hotel's prestige than the actual design of the room.

If he put aside his opinions and considered the attachment people had to Elliott's original vision, then there might be a case to be made for taking a more moderate approach to the renovations than he'd originally planned. He wasn't normally big on compromise, but instinct told him Olivia was a key asset for this project and that her personal commitment to The Mansion would ensure that only the highest standards were maintained.

He'd be hard-pressed to find anyone who'd be more determined to make it succeed than her.

"Would you be willing to stay in charge if we took a more conservative approach to the renovation? I'm not making any promises, but I'm willing to look at different possibilities."

"You're giving me another chance?" she asked, her surprise evident.

He nodded. She hadn't had to come clean, but she had, and he respected that. It also made a difference that her deceit came out of love for her grandfather—not out of any ill-intent or desire to see the project fail. After this talk, he believed she'd be more conscientious about her bias going forward.

"As long as you understand what needs to be done, and I think you do," he said as he gestured towards her plans. She had some really good, viable ideas when she wasn't solely thinking about preserving her grandfather's work. He'd just have to keep a close eye on her. If he ever got the sense that she was putting her grandfather's memory ahead of the hotel's future, he'd replace her. He'd invested a lot into this project and simply couldn't afford to let it fail. "And please cc me on all communications with the architect."

"Of course. Thank you, and I'd love to stay on."

## CHAPTER FIVE

"Hey, Olivia. It's great to be working with you again," Seth Tanner said as he shook her hand. The architect was meeting with the team to discuss specific ideas for the hotel before he made more detailed concept designs.

Olivia forced a smile. "Thanks. It's great to be working with you again, too," she lied. While she liked Seth as a person, she wasn't looking forward to all the disagreements they'd have in the coming months.

Although she'd resigned herself to the scale of renovation Adam wanted, she still planned to fight to keep certain aspects of her grandfather's hotel like the lobby's painted ceiling. But she wouldn't demand too much. Her position on the project was already on perilous ground and she didn't want to do anything that'd make Adam regret his decision to keep her on.

"Okay. Now I know you're lying," the architect said as he released her hand, and she winced.

"How could you tell?"

Seth laughed. "The last time we worked together, you couldn't stop complimenting my work the moment you saw it. Yeah, you wanted to change a few things, but you were practically gushing about how much you liked the designs. It might be my pride talking, but I basically got crickets from you this time around. What's wrong. Don't you like the designs?"

"I do like them," she said, then shrugged, hesitating. "I'm just not sure it's right for The Mansion."

"Because of your grandfather," Seth said knowingly, and she frowned.

"I wouldn't say that." His statement made it seem as if she only wanted to preserve The Mansion's current design because of sentimentality. "I genuinely like the classic beauty of the hotel and was hoping for something more along the lines of a restoration than an outright overhaul and renovation." She'd wager that a lot of people preferred the current design. Why else would so many people stay at the hotel when there were cheaper and more modern ones nearby? "But my dad and Adam want it gutted and redone."

"Just the inside," Adam commented as he walked into the meeting room, with Ricky trailing behind him. "I think the hotel has one of the best exteriors in the whole city. I wouldn't have bought it otherwise," he said, surprising her. Though she'd known he'd wanted to keep the exterior facade, she hadn't known he'd liked it that much.

"You must be Adam Campbell." Seth stepped forward and offered his hand. "I'm Seth Tanner."

"It's nice to meet you. I really like your modern take on the lobby and am looking forward to working with you."

Olivia inwardly sighed as she remembered Seth's plans for the lobby. This meeting was going to be pure hell. "Since we're on the subject, we might as well start."

* * *

"I don't like the idea of an open kitchen in the restaurant," Adam said. "I don't think chefs appreciate having people watch them while they work. I know I wouldn't."

"All right, so we don't have to put the kitchen here then," Seth said as he made an X in the sketch and started drawing inside it. "We could have a more traditional layout with a connecting bar outside."

"Sounds good to me," Olivia piped in when Adam remained silent. Finally, Adam nodded. *Thankfully.* The past hour had been a lot of negotiating amongst the stakeholders about what could or couldn't be in the final design. There'd been a few tense moments, but everyone had kept calm. So far.

"Now, this is what I had in mind for the ballroom." Seth shuffled through his sketches, pulling out the appropriate ones. Olivia held back a frown as she looked at them. He'd wrapped the beautiful columns with wooden panels, boxing in their curves, and removed the connecting arches. He'd also replaced the central rectangular ceiling panel with a pattern of repeating square panels throughout the whole room. It'd definitely make it easier to combine the ballroom with the adjacent meeting rooms if they needed to make the space bigger, but she hated the thought of doing so at the cost of the room's beauty.

She was about to recommend they keep the columns and arches when Adam spoke. "Can I see your ideas for the tearoom?"

"Sure," Seth said as he produced two other sketches. Olivia breathed a sigh of relief when she realized that the changes weren't as significant and encompassing as the ones he'd suggested for the ballroom. The modern design looked more like a lounge or a low-key steakhouse, but at least he'd kept the glass ceiling and stained-glass windows. While the layout was fine, the design wasn't up to par. Perhaps she could hire a separate interior designer to work on that component...

"I'd be interested in seeing fewer renovations in both the ballroom and the tearoom. Could you come up with something that retains more of the original features?" Adam asked after another stretch of silence.

"You would?" Olivia looked up in surprise. She'd been so relieved that he hadn't reported her duplicity to her father that she hadn't pressed him for a response to the revenue breakdowns she'd done on the tearoom and ballroom. But it looked like he was open to listening to alternatives.

"I would."

Seth laughed. "Of course I can, and I know we won't hear any complaints on this end," he said as he pointed towards her. "I'll talk with my guys and let you know what we come up with. Now, the spa..."

Still surprised, Olivia just mouthed, "Thank you," to Adam.

He nodded, acknowledging her.

She knew there was no guarantee that he'd choose Seth's revised concept and that there was a very real chance the spaces would still be completely transformed. But the fact that he'd asked Seth for alternate designs felt like confirmation that there were other people who enjoyed The Mansion's beauty and that it wasn't just sentimentality on her part that made her want to keep the renovations to a minimum.

She might not have the sharpest business acumen, but she'd always had a good sense of design. Feeling as if a burden had been lifted off her, she focused on the rest of Seth's ideas.

# CHAPTER SIX

Adam had just downloaded the updated ballroom designs for The Mansion when his phone rang. Javier Montebello's name flashed on the screen and Adam picked up immediately.

"How's it going down there?" Adam asked. Javier was in charge of the shopping complex they were building in Houston and while Adam was in New York, working on The Mansion, he'd ask Javier to give him daily briefs.

"Not good. Landon's pulled out."

"What? Why?" The family restaurant was a perfect fit for their new complex. People could relax and have a nice meal after they shopped or have a quick bite before they headed to the movie theater. The prices were on the moderate side and, more importantly, the food was fresh and of good quality. In fact, Landon's had been the one to approach them about leasing a spot. And now they wanted to back out? What exactly were they playing at?

"Joe Landon is worried that we'll run into funding problems. They want out so badly they're even willing to pay the lease termination fees."

"Our funding is secured, and we're weeks away from opening the first phase." It didn't make sense. Who went through the trouble of getting all the permits just to cancel right before they started construction? Adam frowned when he remembered Jake's warning about insolvency rumors. "He heard something, didn't he?"

"Yeah. I tried to reassure him, but he wouldn't budge. The good news is that Henry's Roadhouse is willing to take the spot." But they'd have to redo the permits, not to mention alter the design.

"Did he say who he heard the rumor from?" Adam asked, though he already knew.

"He wouldn't say exactly who—just that it was a family member, which was why he gave it so much credence." Javier paused before adding, "I didn't understand it before, but I can see why you hate them so much now."

And he didn't know the half of it. Javier had worked for Adam long enough to see the family tension but hadn't witnessed any acts of outright sabotage such as this one.

What were his parents thinking, trying to ruin his business?

Adam knew he should be grateful that he had another tenant lined up, but right now, he was just plain pissed. He'd worked so hard to build AC Developments into the success that it was and here his parents were, trying to undermine it.

In the past, he would've called Joe Landon to see if he

could ease the man's concerns. But now, he wouldn't waste his breath. If Joe didn't want to work with him, fine. He wasn't going to beg.

Knowing that it wasn't Javier's fault, Adam sighed. "All right. It looks like we'll go with Henry's Roadhouse. Send me the new contract when it's done. Thanks, Javier."

Adam ended the call and contemplated phoning his dad. He didn't want to play into his parents' plan, whatever it was, by initiating contact but, at the same time, he couldn't afford to let them continue scaring off his business partners. He was lucky that the rumors hadn't stopped Jake or Victor from dealing with him and knew he might not be so lucky in the future.

He was just about to call Edward Monroe, a private investigator he often used to track down supplemental information for his business deals, to investigate these rumors when his cell phone rang. He was surprised to see "Dad" flash on the screen and wondered if his dad was calling to rub in his success.

It was crazy to think about how his relationship with his parents had become so strained. Growing up, he'd been the golden child. They'd constantly praised him and bragged about him any chance they got while they'd saved their criticisms and insults for each other and his siblings. But as soon as Adam had moved out of the house and, more importantly, out of their control, Mom and Dad had turned their vitriol on him, too.

Adam didn't want to talk with his dad, but at the same time, he needed to know what he was up against. So, he swiped the screen. He'd learned long ago never to underestimate Mitch Campbell.

"I want these rumors to stop," he answered without preamble. His dad was the king of making roundabout conversations, rarely stating his point outright. Adam had no time for that; he wanted answers and he wanted them now.

"Your mother and I are doing great. Thanks for asking."

Why was Dad talking about Mom as if they got along? Unless they were making the rounds socially, where they pretended to be a loving couple, they could barely stand each other. The only other time they got along was when they were scheming together, which merely increased his worry. What were they up to this time?

"I'm serious, Dad. I want these rumors to stop." If this conversation didn't go anywhere, he'd ask Edward to dig deep into his parents' activities. He hated the thought of stooping to their level, but he needed to even the playing field so that he could counter any further rumors and reduce the risk to his company. It wasn't just money on the line; he had employees to think about as well.

"I don't know what you're talking about."

Adam shook his head. His father never admitted to any wrongdoing—even when the evidence was right in front of him. Why had Adam expected anything different now?

"Can't a father check up on his favorite son without it being anything more?"

*Favorite son?* Yeah, right. That might have been true when he'd been younger. His parents had outright controlled what he'd studied, where he went, who he hung out with… He'd foolishly thought they were trying to do what was best for him and had blindly complied. But now that his eyes had been opened to their true nature, his trust in them had been completely destroyed.

"What do you want, Dad?" Was this *favorite son* rhetoric his dad's way of apologizing or did he have something more sinister planned?

"Nothing. I just wanted to see how you were doing."

Yeah. Sure, he did. "Are you sick?" Maybe Dad was dying and wanted to apologize for everything he and Mom had put Adam and his siblings through. It seemed unlikely, but there was a chance, albeit a tiny one, that he'd repent.

"No."

He frowned. "Is Mom sick?"

"Nobody's sick. I just wanted to say hi. We should have dinner sometime—catch up, you know?"

The conciliatory, slightly pleading tone threw Adam off because it was so out of character for his arrogant father. After brushing off the dinner invite with a vague excuse about having a busy schedule, Adam ended the call and ran a hand through his hair. What exactly was his father up to?

After a few moments of thought, he decided to call the only person who understood his parents—his sister. Martha had the healthiest relationship with their parents, though he knew it wasn't all roses, either. She'd been Mom's second favorite target for her criticisms and anger—their dad being the first. But Martha had never let Mom's behavior bother her—at least not outwardly. She'd always brushed off their cruelty and took the higher ground. Overall, she was much better at handling their parents than him and Doug, who practically relied on Mom and Dad for everything. Hopefully, she could shed some light on their dad's strange call.

Afterwards, he'd call Edward Monroe to ask him to investigate. Adam refused to sit back and wait for his parents' next move, and he refused to lose another customer due to baseless rumors.

# CHAPTER SEVEN

"And this is my proposal for a standard room," Tina Henderson said as she passed Adam and Olivia printouts of the floor plan she'd designed.

After not connecting with the interior design style Seth had proposed, Olivia had reached out to Tina, the interior designer who'd worked on their Vancouver hotel. And judging from this floor plan, she'd made the right decision.

Tina had used the extra space in the guest room to create a division between the sleeping and living areas, practically creating another room. Guests could use the space to entertain their friends, as a mini-office, or even as their own private lounge where they could enjoy a quiet dinner in.

Olivia could see it coming together already. A full marble bathroom with a bathtub and a separate shower, a spacious bedroom, and a living room with a gorgeous view of the Manhattan skyline. It would be perfect for a business traveler or a family with children.

But it seemed Adam had other ideas. "Do we really

need to separate the living room from the bedroom?" he asked.

Olivia frowned as she looked at him. He'd been in a bad mood the entire meeting, finding fault with most of the ideas and speaking in an abrupt, snappish tone. It was almost as if he were gearing for a fight.

"I think so," Tina answered cautiously, as if she'd sensed the same. "The additional living space can provide families with a playroom for the children and business travelers with a separate working area, where they can leave work at work, thereby creating a more pleasant experience."

Adam looked unconvinced but said nothing and went back to examining the plans. A few moments later, he pointed to the living room. "And another chandelier?" he asked as he gestured towards the picture. "It's frivolous and wasteful to put a chandelier in the living room. We're trying to modernize the hotel, not make it more ostentatious."

That was it! Adam could be as much of an asshole as he wanted to his own employees, but he couldn't act that way towards Tina. "Can I speak with you outside?" Olivia gritted out as she stood.

Dark eyes flashed as he glared at her before he followed her out of the room.

She shook with anger. His attitude was totally uncalled for, especially in this meeting, which, as an initial design presentation, was about getting feedback and refining their general ideas.

He didn't get a pass to be rude just because he didn't like Tina's designs. Olivia had no patience with people who took their moods out on others. Especially people like Adam, who were in a position of power. In her mind, people who had authority had a greater responsibility for behaving decently and for treating people with respect.

She'd come to respect and admire Adam's working style. He was always firm and decisive and when a decision was out of his area of expertise, he deferred to the experts. But after his behavior today and the way he was taking his bad mood out on Tina? Well, Olivia's good opinion of him just dropped tenfold.

"What was that?" she asked as soon as the door was closed, and they were a safe distance away so as not to be overheard.

"With chandeliers in the lobby and the restaurant, I think we should tone it down a bit, don't you? Like I said, we're trying to modernize."

"I'll be the first to admit that my grandpa went overboard with the chandeliers—both in terms of the quantity and the style—but Tina has definitely pulled back on those. Besides, you know that we're removing most, if not all, the chandeliers in the lobby." Because no matter what Adam thought, a well-selected chandelier in the right place lent elegance to the overall feel of a space. "My problem is with you. You've been overly critical and, frankly, a pain in the ass." His pettiness was a surprise because she'd started not only to enjoy working with him, but to actually look forward to their interactions. He had good ideas and was usually open-minded. But not today. "I don't know what's gotten into you, but you need to either temper your attitude or leave."

Seconds ticked by as he stared at her, and she began to wonder if she'd made a critical error. She'd never spoken to a client like that, but she liked Tina and appreciated the vision she brought to her work. Adam's behavior had been completely unwarranted.

But had she overstepped?

Adam *had* kept her on the project despite her deceit with Seth's designs and had even agreed to just refresh the ballroom and the tearoom instead of the full-on renovation Seth had originally proposed. But how would he respond to being reprimanded? She couldn't imagine he'd take it in stride.

A sick feeling of anxiety was forming in her stomach when a smile curved his lips. "You know, you're kinda cute when you're mad."

The unexpectedness of his remark caught her off guard. After acting like a truculent child, he was cracking jokes? "Be serious," Olivia finally said. "You can't talk to Tina that way. At least show some respect for her talent and creativity." When he remained silent, she sighed. "If you really don't like the designs, we can find another interior designer." She didn't agree with his criticisms, but hiring another designer was the least she could do after all the concessions he'd made.

"Give me a day or two to think about it," Adam said after another long pause.

"All right."

She rubbed her brow, trying to ease the tension there. These design consults seemed to be going on forever. And yes, part of the reason was because they'd changed some of the parameters of the original design brief. But another contributing factor was that there were just so many people weighing in on the initial presentations. Usually, a smaller group of people saw the initial designs, offered feedback to refine the concepts, and then presented a more cohesive design to the shareholders. But unlike Montgomery's usual clients, Adam was involved at every stage.

"You know, you don't have to attend all these meetings, right?" she asked after a second. It was probably why he was so irritated. There were so many discussions happening—they were constantly discarding old ideas and brainstorming new ones. Oftentimes, they even revisited ideas they'd already tossed out.

So much back and forth was going on at these early stages that, unless you understood the process, seemed like you were going around in circles. Their clients usually relied on Montgomery's project team to handle all these smaller details, preferring to see the plans in the later stages before offering their opinions. Montgomery's expertise was one of the main reasons why hotel owners hired them, after all.

"I can promise not to make any big decisions without your approval," she continued, guessing that Adam didn't trust her, which was fair enough. She wouldn't either if she were in his shoes.

"I appreciate the offer, but I want to be involved in these early stages."

"Then I hope you'll keep your attitude in check," she said without thinking, and he grinned.

"All right."

His sudden agreeableness worried her, but all she could do was hope that he'd maintain this calmer demeanor for the rest of the meeting with Tina. She nodded before heading back to the meeting room.

* * *

"How about something like this?" Tina asked as Adam and Olivia walked into the room.

Adam took the proffered tablet and paper. The image on the tablet showed a rectangular-shaped lamp held up by the corners, while the plan showed possible placement in the room. The lamp seemed like a good fit for the design of the room and, although it was difficult to tell from the picture, the dimensions seemed right for the proportions of the space.

"There'd be enough light if you open the window shades during the day without it," Tina said. "But it won't be sufficient during the nights and winters. There'll have to be auxiliary lighting elsewhere."

"It's better," he said as he handed the sheet and tablet to Olivia. He'd see how he felt about it tomorrow, when his head was clearer.

"I do think chandeliers would be a nice touch for the two-floor suites, though," Tina commented.

"Oh, and we could repeat the rectangular design in the lobby," Olivia said, obviously liking the idea.

Adam watched them talk, the two women clearly understanding each other's opinions if their nodding and open body language were any indication, and inwardly sighed. He hadn't meant to take his frustration out on Tina, and had, in fact, thought he'd been keeping his emotions firmly in check.

But the foul mood he'd been in ever since he'd spoken with his father last night had obviously seeped out. He hated not knowing what his parents were up to. It was as if he were constantly waiting for the other shoe to drop. And the more he thought about everything, the more frustrated he got.

The reason for his dad's call still baffled him. Why hadn't Dad gloated about the impact those rumors had on AC Developments? For that matter, why had Dad pretended not to know anything about the lies? If Adam didn't know better, he would've thought his parents were trying to get on his good side by suggesting they have dinner together. Even Martha hadn't believed that Dad had wanted to catch up sometime and had promptly invited herself to the meal whenever it took place.

Adam really hoped he wouldn't have to meet his parents. Despite their strained relationship, he'd always done his best to act civil towards them. But telling outright lies about him and threatening his business was too much, especially when he didn't know what their endgame was. Still, if a dinner did occur, he'd be grateful for Martha's support. Her presence would ensure he didn't do or say something he'd regret.

Recognizing that these thoughts were making him broody, he shook them off and focused on what Olivia and Tina were talking about. They were now discussing the bathroom sizes of the various rooms and how to adapt the fixtures to outfit each one with both a tub and a stand-alone shower. At the mention of rain showerheads and body jets, his mind pictured Olivia in a cloud of steam and his gaze dipped to Olivia's lips.

He'd had the crazy urge to kiss her in the hallway and probably would have if not for the fact that they were in the middle of the office. She'd just looked so damn sexy when she'd gotten all riled up. Her flushed cheeks and passion-filled eyes had struck him dumb.

Considering she was his new business partner's daughter, it was a good thing he hadn't given in to the urge. He didn't want to do anything that would put him on Victor's bad side or make the man pull out of the deal.

Still, Adam couldn't stop himself from wondering what would've happened if he had kissed Olivia. Would she have gone all soft on him or would she have pulled away, flashing those beautiful, angry eyes at him?

He wasn't imagining the undercurrent of attraction between them—an attraction that only grew stronger the more he got to know her. He couldn't remember ever being so drawn to someone before and the fact that she'd had the guts to talk to him in a way no one did had immediately spiked his interest and made him want her even more.

As if she'd heard his thoughts, Olivia glanced at him. He winked and she narrowed her eyes at him before answering Tina. In a way he chose not to examine too closely, his mood immediately improved. He'd much rather think about Olivia than his parents' tiresome behavior. With that decision made, he knew that he was going to enjoy the rest of the meeting.

* * *

"Thank you for dialing it back in there," Olivia said once the meeting was over and Tina was gone.

"I'm sorry. I've been in a bad mood ever since I spoke with my father yesterday. I shouldn't have taken it out on anyone." He'd apologize to Tina the next time he saw her.

"At least I know I'm not the only one who gets driven crazy by parents."

If she only knew. Her dad was a saint compared to his, though he guessed one could never tell from a person's public persona. His own parents did their best to appear as if they were the perfect couple. They sat on countless charity boards and were charming as can be. But in their private lives, they were vipers.

"Have dinner with me," he said suddenly. He didn't know if it was because he enjoyed her company or if he just didn't want to think about his parents for a while longer, but he really wanted to go out with her.

It took her a second before she nodded. "All right."

A tightness he hadn't known was there eased in his chest. "Great. I'll drive."

# CHAPTER EIGHT

"So, do you want something more in line with the designs Seth's firm did instead of what Tina brought today?" Olivia asked as she cut into her steak.

A smile tugged at Adam's lips. It was the first time he'd had dinner with a woman who kept trying to steer the conversation towards business. It was usually the other way around, with women trying to turn a business meeting into something more. Perhaps it was because he wasn't a real estate mogul or a billionaire to Olivia like he'd been to those other women. Since her family was probably just as rich as—if not richer than—his, he was just another guy to her. The thought was surprisingly freeing.

"No. Tina's was definitely better. I'll take a look at her designs tomorrow and let you know what I decide."

"Thanks."

He nodded at her. "Do you have any other projects in the works?" he asked as he dug into his meal.

"Well... I'm hoping to open a hotel near Yosemite," she

said after a few seconds. "I feel like there's a huge opportunity for luxury hotels in areas where outdoor activities are the main draw. The existing ones are all around the same places like Jackson Hole or Lake Tahoe and are often fully booked a year in advance. I'm hoping we can fill that gap." She lifted a shoulder. "Just because someone likes hiking or kayaking doesn't mean that they wouldn't appreciate all the luxurious amenities an upscale hotel provides. In fact, they'd probably value it more. At the end of a long day, they could get a massage at the spa or have a quiet night in while enjoying the fantastic views from their private balcony."

Her eyes lit up as she began talking about how the hotel could work with family reunions and corporate retreats and he couldn't help but be entranced. She was always beautiful, but somehow, seeing her so passionate about her plans made her even more so.

"On top of having a grab and go station that sells sandwiches and the like for people to bring for the day, we could have a restaurant with a rotating menu. Most people won't venture far from the hotel at night and I want to give them the choice of menu options in addition to the various restaurants."

He'd never thought about the tourism near national parks before, but it figured there'd be an underserved market for luxury hotels. Most of the hotels near the parks were on the lower end of the amenities scale and he was sure many guests would appreciate having another option.

Olivia's shoulders suddenly slumped. "Of course, my

dad hasn't approved it yet, but I feel like this is the one he'll finally approve."

"He's rejected your ideas before?" The thought was surprising. From all their interactions, she'd seemed really knowledgeable about the hotel industry—certainly more so than he was—and smart, too.

"Yes, though they weren't all like this. This is my second attempt at pitching one of these outdoor adventurer-type hotels. Before that, I wanted to open hotels targeted towards young professionals. They're the fastest growing market in the hospitality industry right now."

"Did he give a reason for the rejections?"

"Everything from the hotel not quite being the right fit for the Montgomery brand to overestimating the willingness of people to pay for a luxury hotel." She smiled. "Though I still disagree with my dad on a lot of his points, I admit I got caught up in the excitement of wanting to make my mark on the company and may have been a little premature in all the excitement. But I've learned a lot since that first rejection and have incorporated a lot of what I've learned into this new proposal."

He couldn't help but think that her loss was his gain. If one of her proposals had been approved, she wouldn't have been assigned to The Mansion, and he would've never gotten the chance to get to know her. Because no matter what he thought about her and her hang-ups, he enjoyed working with her.

"Did you ever think about striking out on your own?" Why had she stayed despite her dad's rejections? He was sure she would've been able to get the backers needed to pursue her projects, but instead, she was dreaming up new ideas to submit.

"I don't want to break away from the family business. It'd never even occurred to me as an option. I want to grow Montgomery Hotels the way my dad did, and I think that a small chain of these hotels is the way to go. It would really enhance our portfolio and give people who wouldn't have otherwise tried one of our hotels a taste of what we do." She smiled. "And then hopefully, they'll want to try our other properties in the future."

Seeing her so optimistic tugged at his heart. Even in the face of rejection, she was so damn cheerful and was even looking forward to future opportunities. He didn't think he'd ever been so optimistic. Driven to succeed, yes, but that had mostly stemmed from wanting to show his parents that he didn't need them while she didn't seem to have an ounce of hard feelings towards her dad for his rejections. Her heart was pure in a way he doubted he'd ever seen before. Even when she'd lied about the architect's designs, she'd been thinking about her grandfather—not herself.

Remembering that, he thought of earlier, when she'd offered to take care of the small things and to only involve him when it came to the bigger decisions and knew he couldn't risk it. Sure, she had some wonderful ideas for The Mansion and was doing a great job, overall, but her love for her family made her blind to what the hotel really needed. Hell. He could still remember her hesitation when she'd looked at the concept designs during their last meeting with Axe. She'd probably thought she'd been doing a good job of hiding her reaction, but he'd seen the panic in her eyes.

And because of that, he knew there was no way he could leave any stage of the design process, no matter how small, to her.

"How about your siblings?" he asked. "Do they work with the company as well?"

"I only have one—a brother. He decided to go into the original family business—banking. He never did like working in the hotel."

"Let me guess, your dad made you two work in the hotel."

She nodded. "Every day, after school. He wanted us to learn the business inside and out the way he had. We did everything from cleaning rooms to taking reservations."

He smiled. He could just imagine a young Olivia working the front desk. "And I'm guessing you fell in love with the work?"

"No. I absolutely hated it," she said with so much conviction that he laughed. "It didn't seem fair that my classmates got to go shopping after school while I was stuck with hotel duties."

"What changed?" Because she obviously enjoyed it now.

"Honestly? I never intended to end up in the hospitality industry. I studied architecture in college."

"Architecture, really? That's quite a departure from hotels."

"I've always been intrigued by buildings and their designs. They're such a fundamental part of our lives and yet time and time again, there are these amazing architects who can take the most basic elements—walls, openings, rooves—and bring something entirely new to the table.

And there's something beautiful about generation after generation enjoying the same building—taking delight in the same spaces. Once I started studying deeper, I began to see that a wall was more than just a wall—that we could go beyond the limits of our own boundaries. And that—" She gave a little laugh. "Sorry, I can get a little carried away."

"No, I like that perspective. Even though architecture plays a big part in what I do, I've never really thought of the structures beyond their functional purposes." Seeing her so passionate reminded him of his grandfather and the way he could talk for hours about different chemicals and how he'd come up with the perfect process and combination for a new product. Excitement just oozed off the both of them and he couldn't help but think that Grandpa would've loved Olivia.

Adam doubted he'd ever be able to look at the design of one of his complexes again without thinking of the enthusiasm in Olivia's voice, encouraging him to see a greater purpose to what he built, although his managers would probably think he'd gone crazy if he ever talked about the building's meaning beyond its cost per square foot.

"You clearly love architecture. Why did you leave it?"

Several beats passed, where she looked unsure of what to say. Finally, she started, "I really struggled in Studio, which unfortunately, was the most important class." She lifted a shoulder. "No matter how hard I worked on my designs, I barely passed. Three years into the curriculum, my dad had a heart attack and my parents asked me to help out in the office. Since the attack was stress-related, Mom sided with the doctors, who said Dad couldn't go rushing back to work. Of course, Dad wasn't too happy about that, but Mom knew that he'd be more comfortable if either Robert or me was at the office, keeping an eye out on things and keeping him abreast of what was happening. At the time, the thought of two more years of Studio was pure torture so I jumped at the opportunity to take a break. I told myself that I would go back to school once Dad recovered, but I never did."

"Do you ever think about going back?"

"Sometimes, but I just can't see how it would fit in with my work at Montgomery. I really love working with the company, but at the same time, I don't see myself ever becoming as good at architecture as someone like Seth. And I've got enough pride that I wouldn't want to be anything less than the best." She laughed. "It's funny. Growing up, I always did my best to excel in school so that I wouldn't have to work for Montgomery and now I love it."

Adam laughed. "Since your early hotel duties were basically chores, it's understandable."

She nodded at him. "How about you? Did you ever think about joining Dannier?" she asked, referring to the cosmetics company his grandfather had started.

"Almost my whole life," he said, and she blinked in surprise. He laughed. He knew what she was thinking. What he was doing now was just about the complete opposite. "I even wanted to major in chemistry to understand the products more," he confessed. "I'd always loved watching the machines at the factory, but something just clicked inside of me the first time my grandfather took me to his lab, and I knew that that was what I wanted to do.

But my dad had other plans. He wanted me to study business." Sometimes, Adam still couldn't believe the lengths his father would go to force him to do his bidding. And his mother was just as bad. "Eventually, I realized that I couldn't work with him."

Even without all his dad's lies, Adam knew they never would've been able to work together for long. When he was seventeen, he'd approached his dad about starting a men's care product line. He knew men bought their products, but it was oftentimes a source of embarrassment, because their cream was best known as a moisturizer for women. Dad had called the idea intriguing, but had shut it down, claiming men could just order their moisturizer online. He hadn't even spared a thought to all the additional products they could've made.

Though Adam would've never had Olivia's patience to stay at the company after multiple rejections, he sometimes wondered what would've happened if he had stayed. Would he have eventually been able to convince Dad to develop a men's line or even just an aftershave? And would that one product have eventually led to a whole product line?

"That must've been hard," Olivia said. "But I guess it's better to have come to the realization sooner rather than later and to save that relationship. And you've made such a name for yourself in the real estate development. I'm sure your parents must be proud."

If only. "Actually, they're still mad at me for going my own way," he said before he could think better of it. "Since I was the first-born son, they thought it was my duty to take over eventually."

"How long has it been since you left and started AC Developments?

"Around twelve years."

Her eyes widened. "Twelve years and they still haven't gotten over the fact that you left?"

He shrugged. "They have a long memory."

"But that's insane. How about your siblings? Are they working at the company?"

"No. My sister loves her job as an IP lawyer and my brother doesn't exactly have the discipline to work. But hopefully, as time goes on, they'll take more active roles and join the board of directors." Because no matter what had happened between him and his parents, Adam wanted Dannier to stay under his family's control. It was their legacy.

Olivia frowned and he couldn't help but think about how different her experience had been. Unlike her, he used to live for the days his grandpa would take him to the factory and when he'd gotten older, he'd wanted nothing more than to work at the family's business. Now, he didn't even talk with his parents unless he had to.

"How did you get into land development?" she asked, breaking the silence. "It's quite a change from chemical research."

He laughed. "At the time, I just wanted to make my own money so that I could become self-sufficient as fast as I could. If I'd gone through with chemical research, I would've had to get a college degree before I could find work, or I would've had to create my own business. And since I didn't have any bright ideas for a new product, I thought of real estate. It had seemed like a bullet-proof idea at the time. It wasn't until later that I realized all the ways it could've gone wrong." Especially since he'd had absolutely no idea of what he'd been doing and had no construction experience at all. Sure, he'd done a lot of research, but real-life application was always different.

"I can imagine! But why Texas? Do you have family there?"

"Nope. No relatives." He'd had to do everything himself. "I'm sure you've read those articles about the booming economy in Texas and how a lot of businesses were moving down there. And since people follow the jobs, I figured any housing community or shopping complex in the right location would be a success. I made a map of the developments I knew were in the pipes and flew to Dallas. I drove around to see what opportunities I could find. Afterwards, I drove down to Austin and did the same thing. I eventually bought the development rights to a large piece of land just outside of Houston using the money my grandfather left me and started out with a small, twenty-house community and a five-store shopping complex."

He'd been really lucky to find a wonderful architect from the get-go, but his choice in construction companies had been subpar. He'd patted himself on the back when he'd found one that was experienced and reasonably priced. But they'd turned around and subcontracted the work to an unreliable crew. After they'd missed a few deadlines, Adam had moved to Texas to oversee the project himself and had even done twice-a-day inspections with the architect to make sure everything went as planned. Adam now had his dream team in place, but it had taken a steep learning curve.

"We got tenants for the shopping complex almost as soon as we broke ground and sold all the houses before we even had the chance to set up a model home. We had a short delay in building, but thankfully, we didn't lose any tenants or buyers. The proceeds then went to building an extension of the community."

"And you've succeeded magnificently and in such a short time!"

"I was incredibly lucky that my grandfather left me a trust fund and even more so, that he didn't make me wait to access the money." Because of that, Adam had been able to branch out on his own without his parents' help.

Olivia laughed. "The money would've probably afforded you a lifetime of luxury and instead, you did this, risking it all."

"You could say the same of yourself. I'm sure you have enough to last a lifetime, too, and yet you choose to work."

She wrinkled her nose. "Character deficiency. I've never been the smart one. What's your excuse?"

He smiled, then shrugged. "I just knew I didn't want to be like the other trust-fund babies who basically do nothing." He wanted more for himself than the idle life many of his old schoolmates had chosen. The fact that his parents had been waiting for him to fail had only strengthened his resolve to do something more with his life. "My grandpa was a self-made man and seeing how he worked—the products he made and the opportunities he gave to his employees—made me want to do something similar. I had classmates whose families relied solely on investments for their income and I thought it was such a crazy way to live. They weren't doing anything and yet they were making more money than my grandfather's hard-working employees. Though my grandpa never told me how to use the money, I know he would've been disappointed if I'd chosen to live off it instead of making something of myself."

Once he was done, Adam was surprised at how much he'd said. He'd never opened up to someone as much as he had to her—especially about work and money. He'd always been cautious with his words, but he had a gut feeling she felt the same way.

"How about you?" he asked. "And don't say it's a character deficiency."

She laughed, then nodded. "My dad. He really drilled into my brother and me how lucky we were. He was always saying how fortunate we were to be able to eat what we wanted and to buy this or that, and that we shouldn't complain about having to work at the hotel." His lips twitched and she continued, "And I think growing up in the hotel the way we did made work seem like second nature. But as I grew older, I realized how blessed I was to be given so many amazing opportunities and I just knew that I couldn't let them go to waste."

Adam couldn't help but admire her work ethic. He could easily imagine someone like her—who'd been forced to work at an early age—taking the first opportunity to not work, to finally have a break. But not her. Not only did she want to earn her own way in the world, she also wanted to make a difference like he did. He didn't think he'd ever met a woman like her and wished they'd met under different circumstances, which just spoke to how crazy she made him.

She was doing an amazing job on The Mansion and here he was, thinking about how great things could've been between them if they didn't work together. He inwardly shook his head. He'd always made business his top priority, but Olivia was wrecking his concentration.

He should just be happy that he had someone like her on his team and make do with only seeing her in business settings. But he soon found himself wondering if tomorrow was too soon to invite her for another "business dinner."

* * *

"Thanks for dinner," Olivia said as Adam parked next to her car.

"How about thanking me with dinner tomorrow night?" he asked, and she laughed. She would love to go out with him on a real date, but knew he had to be joking. With how much she'd talked about herself, there was no way he'd enjoyed tonight. But as usual, he was being his charming and flirtatious self.

She didn't know what was wrong with her. She should've used the dinner to impress him with her ideas for the renovation. Instead, she'd talked about her struggles in school and her rejected proposals.

He'd just been so easy to talk with that she'd forgotten

herself. He'd seemed really interested and had asked these thought-provoking questions that had her opening up in a way she rarely did. There was something about him—perhaps in the way he looked at her, as though he were seeing the real her—that made her feel as if they were the only two people in the room. She hadn't wanted the dinner to end.

It had been so easy to forget that he was a client and not someone she'd known all her life. And that was a dangerous line of thinking, because she could really fall for him. If she were being completely honest, she'd already begun to.

What he'd achieved in business was nothing short of admirable and she got the sense that he really cared about his employees. But no matter what she'd felt tonight, he was a client. Nothing could happen between them, so she'd just have to watch herself around him and make sure she kept her attraction—and mouth—in check.

Eager to get their conversation on a more even business-footing, she tucked her hair behind her ear and said, "So, let me know what you decide on the interior design."

"I will," he said, then slid his palm against her cheek and kissed her. His lips were unexpectedly soft, and she found herself kissing him back. Pleasure tore through her as his tongue slid against hers, deepening the kiss. Too soon, it was over, and she resisted the urge to pull his head down for more.

*Okay, so he hadn't been joking about dinner tomorrow.*

Warmth spread through her at the realization that he'd enjoyed her company before reality set in. Though her dad had floated the idea of setting her up with Adam, she knew he'd just been teasing. In reality, any relationship between her and Adam would be highly improper, and she would never deliberately do anything that would reflect poorly on Montgomery. The fact that her dad had never explicitly forbidden her from mixing business with pleasure only strengthened her resolve. Her dad trusted her to do the right thing. She couldn't pay him back by betraying that trust.

Besides, it was hard enough to stay objective when it came to The Mansion. Getting involved with Adam would unnecessarily complicate matters—especially when they were at such odds regarding the design. Still, she couldn't help wishing things were different. She couldn't remember ever being so in tune with someone.

Shivers ran down her spine when she looked up and saw the expression in his eyes. They were smoldering. "We shouldn't have done that," she said when she finally found her voice. Even so, she knew she'd be reliving that kiss over and over again tonight.

He nodded as he watched her. "Probably, but I wouldn't mind doing it again."

Neither would she and that was the problem. She'd felt a connection to him that she'd never felt with anyone before and because of that, she was tempted to throw caution to the wind. But she couldn't afford any more mistakes. She'd already messed up big time by withholding Seth's concepts and needed to prove to herself that she could handle the project.

"But we should," she answered him. "I doubt either one

of us would feel comfortable seeing each other when things ended, but we'd have to for work." With him being such an active partner, it was a recipe for disaster. Their dealings would only be that much harder to navigate and she didn't want to do anything that would jeopardize The Mansion deal or her position in it. No matter how amicable a split would be, it would still be awkward.

Adam sighed as he leaned against his seat and ran a hand down his face. "Okay. I get it."

Disappointment bit at her at his easy acceptance before she cursed herself. She hadn't actually wanted him to argue with her, had she? Opportunities like The Mansion only came once in a lifetime. She wouldn't screw it up—no matter how good of a kisser Adam was or how connected she'd felt to him tonight.

# CHAPTER NINE

He should've never kissed Olivia.

Adam sighed as he headed towards her office Thursday morning. She'd said things could get awkward if they dated, then broke up. But somehow, without them ever dating, things were already awkward. She'd barely been able to look him in the eye during yesterday's meeting and frankly, he'd been no better. If he hadn't been looking at her lips, he'd been staring at his notepad, trying not to remember how sweet she'd tasted.

Before things got worse, he'd decided to give her a peace offering in the hopes of getting their relationship back on a friendly but professional footing. Because he simply couldn't afford another disaster like yesterday. The usually talkative and knowledgeable Olivia had barely spoken, and he'd been just as distracted, leading to quite an unproductive meeting. If it hadn't been for their supporting team members guiding the discussions, they wouldn't have gotten anything done.

Though he didn't like it, he knew that Olivia had made the right decision. Turning a business relationship into something more was always messy, which was why he'd always avoided it. Not to mention the fact that they both had very different views on how to approach the renovations. They'd probably always be second-guessing each other or wondering if one was using the other.

It was a damn shame.

He would've loved the chance to get to know her better, but there was too much riding on this project for them to mess it up with a fling. Hopefully, this visit would diffuse the awkwardness between them. He'd called the receptionist to ask if there was any dessert Olivia particularly liked, and now, here he was with a cake from her favorite bakery.

His grandfather had always told him that a small present could go a long way towards softening someone up. Quite often, Grandpa would forget the time when he was experimenting in the lab and wouldn't get home until the following morning. To make it up to Grandma, Grandpa would stop at whatever store was open to buy a bouquet of flowers or a baked treat. Grandma had been all too familiar with Grandpa's forgetfulness, but she'd still been pleased that he'd thought enough of her to bring an apology gift.

Praying that Grandpa's advice would work on Olivia, Adam knocked on her open door. She looked up from the paper she'd been writing on and froze.

"Hey," she said stiffly, and he couldn't help but miss the

easiness between them. It was probably too much to expect things to go back to the way they were before the kiss, and he was surprised by the sense of loss he felt.

A part of him wished he'd never kissed her. Not only had he jeopardized a business relationship, but possibly a budding friendship as well. He'd found a kindred spirit in her and hated that she was now uncomfortable around him. But another part of him knew that he'd had to try, or he would've always regretted it. Because regardless of his worries about how it would affect their work, he was still willing to risk a relationship with her. If only she were willing. But she'd made her decision and he'd abide by it.

"Hey, Olivia. I just wanted to drop off this cake," he said as he approached.

Her eyes widened as she accepted the box. "Thank you. I love Dawn's."

As she moved aside the papers she'd been working on to make room for the cake, he glanced down and saw a sketch. It looked like a lobby, but with its rustic, cabin-like features, it was obviously not The Mansion.

"Is that your Yosemite hotel?"

She froze, her cheeks turning a cute pink. "Yeah. Even though my dad hasn't approved of it yet, I still like thinking about it and working out some of the kinks."

"It looks good." The stone fireplace and earth-toned palette created a charming and inviting space. He could easily imagine settling into one of the leather chairs with a hot drink. He was tempted to tease her about architecture school, but didn't. Doing so spoke of a familiarity, an intimacy between them that was better left untouched. Yeah, there were sparks, but he wouldn't fan them no matter how much he was itching to. He'd come here today in the hopes of resurrecting their professional relationship—not make it worse.

He motioned towards one of the chairs across her desk. "May I?" She nodded and he sat. He sighed as he ran a hand down his thighs. "I wanted to clear the air and say that there are no hard feelings."

Amusement lit her eyes. "It would be petty if you did have any. We're working on a really important project and can't afford to have any distractions." The mixture of seriousness and lightheartedness—so similar to his own personality—reminded him of why he was so drawn to her. "I think yesterday's meeting gave us a little sense of how things would've been."

"That's actually why I came here today. Yesterday was awful."

She winced. "I know, and I apologize. This project deserves my full attention, and I didn't give that yesterday."

"There's no need to apologize. I wasn't any better and I'm beginning to see the wisdom of your decision." He'd already had trouble concentrating after simply kissing her. He could just imagine how useless he'd be in a meeting if they ever did more than kiss. "I've been wracking my brain, thinking of how we should move forward, and all I could think of was getting you a cake to head off a possible stand-off."

"Which I totally appreciate," she said, and he smiled.

"Any ideas on how we should proceed?" Even if there could never be anything between them, he still wanted the Olivia who wasn't afraid to tear him a new one or to tell him to dial back his attitude.

"Well. I'm hoping the awkwardness will pass with time. Perhaps it was just because it was the first time seeing each other after the kiss that made things so hard? We certainly seem to be doing better now. Hey, how about this—we can eat the cake while we go over the things we should've talked about at the meeting if we hadn't been so distracted?"

"I distract you?" His chest warmed at the thought.

"You know you do."

"I know, but I wanted to hear you say it."

She laughed. "Anyways, some thoughts and ideas popped into my head as I was going over the notes I plan to send to Tina. I was going to email Ricky later today, but we could go over them now."

Relief filled him at the knowledge that she was willing to push through the awkwardness between them. He'd worried that he'd made a mistake that couldn't be undone.

"I'd like that."

"Great. Let me just get the plates and utensils."

* * *

Olivia made her way through the familiar restaurant, admiring its unique mix of American Craftsman and Modern architecture. With its warm lights and simple woodwork, The Tavern pulled off an elegant coziness few could compare to.

It was still early in the night, so there wasn't much of a crowd, but from experience, she knew every table would be occupied by the time she and Stacy left. Stacy had called earlier, asking if she was available for dinner. Given how busy she'd been at work, Olivia was glad for the chance to step away from it all for a bit.

She found her friend at their usual table, off to the side of the restaurant and away from the main dining room. "Hey, Stacy!" she said as she approached.

"Livie!" Stacy smiled as she put her phone down and stood to hug her.

Remembering Stacy's bodyguard, Pete, Olivia looked at his spot—two tables away—and gave him a short nod. The bodyguard was a constant reminder of how Stacy had been kidnapped and ransomed when they were younger. After Stacy had been returned safely, her parents had never let her out without protection again. Remembering that scary time, Olivia tightened her hold on her friend before releasing her.

"So, are we celebrating anything?" Olivia asked as they sat.

"No, but that reminds me. The grand opening for our community center in Trenton is next Saturday."

"Oh. I can't wait to see how everything turned out." They'd only been laying the beams the last time she'd visited the site.

"Here, I'll show you the pictures." Stacy grabbed her phone and opened the photo album. "Thanks again for all your help with the design," she said as she handed her the phone.

"It was nothing." While they'd been having dinner one evening, Stacy had talked about her vision for the shelter. Olivia had begun absentmindedly sketching on a napkin and by the time dinner was over, she'd had a purse full of napkins and a head full of designs.

Over the next few weeks, they'd worked together on making the concepts and had even visited a few other centers to see what was needed and what could be improved.

Olivia scrolled through the photos in awe. It felt incredible to see her designs come to life. Sure, she'd given ideas and suggestions on hotel renovations, but they were just that—suggestions. It wasn't like this community center where the library had a separate entrance in the back and the toddlers' play corner was right next to the dining hall because she'd put them there. She'd really enjoyed the challenge of doing something different and was glad her hard work had paid off. The center looked amazing.

"It's not nothing," Stacy said. "On top of you saving us a ton of money, I don't think anyone else would've been as patient with me."

Olivia laughed. "It would help if you'd stopped relying on volunteers." Stacy was amazing at getting people to donate their money, but she stretched out every dollar to the last penny. Every dollar saved, she said, was another dollar she could use to buy food or clothes. The problem was that she relied heavily on volunteers, many of whom had other priorities.

"I know, I know! I hired an architect and a construction company this time, didn't I?"

"Because there was literally no building this time," Olivia answered dryly. The charity Stacy was involved with usually renovated existing buildings to suit their needs. But this time, someone had donated an empty lot and, instead of selling it, the board had decided to build a community center.

"You did," Olivia said, smiling. "I still can't believe Megan Carlyle volunteered her nephew's services for that center in Queens without asking him." It was one thing to do a little plumbing work and another to knock down some walls and build a commercial-sized kitchen.

"I *did* try to say no, but she was really persistent. Anyway, I think she's learned her—"

"Good evening, Ms. Montgomery, it's good to see you again," Derek, their waiter, interrupted and poured a glass of wine for Olivia.

Olivia thanked the man and turned to Stacy, "Do you know what you want yet?" Though Olivia wasn't late, she didn't want to make her friend wait longer than she already had.

Stacy nodded. "Derek recommended the snapper."

"Make it two then," Olivia said as she handed him her menu.

Once the waiter left, Stacy asked, "How about you? Is Adam Campbell still giving you a hard time?"

Olivia winced when she remembered all the bad things she'd said about Adam when she'd first been assigned to the project. "He's not as bad as I originally thought," she admitted. "You know how he agreed to restore the tearoom and the ballroom after I ran those numbers you recommended. There've been a few differences of opinions since then and I'm always surprised by how willing he is to listen. More so than I am, though I am doing my best to change that. All in all, he's been a really great partner."

A beat passed before Stacy started, "Oh my goodness. You like him."

Olivia was about to deny it before she remembered she was talking with Stacy. Her best friend would never betray her trust. "I do," she admitted. "I think I started falling for him when he agreed to keep the tearoom. He didn't have to do that and considering the way I acted before, he had absolutely no reason to. And yet, he did." She shook her head softly. "I just don't know how we're going to be able to work together. Everything's been so awkward since the kiss."

Stacy's eyebrows rose. "Was this before or after he agreed to keep the tearoom?"

Olivia's cheeks warmed. "After. We had dinner a few weeks ago and he kissed me when he was dropping me off to my car."

She still cringed when she thought about all the personal details she'd revealed that night. Her feelings towards him had begun warming since he'd let her stay on the project, but he'd turned out to be so much more than she'd expected.

Unfortunately for her, the more she liked someone, the less of a filter she had.

"Afterwards, I told him I didn't want to mess up our

business relationship, but the next meeting was a complete disaster. I couldn't concentrate on a word being said. All I could think about was that kiss." Though admittedly, she'd been thinking about that kiss a lot. It'd just been unfortunate that he'd been in the room at that time. "I'm pretty sure I had a blush burning my face throughout the whole meeting. He brought cake the next—"

"He brought you cake?"

"He did." No matter how sweet and thoughtful she'd thought the gesture, she knew he'd only done so to save their working relationship. He simply hadn't wanted another disastrous meeting.

"I wish someone would bring me cake."

Olivia smiled and said, "Anyway, he seemed eager to get things back to the way they were, but he hasn't come to a meeting since." She'd been looking forward to seeing him again and had been disappointed when he hadn't shown up. "Ricky, his second in command, says that Adam's busy in Houston, working on a new complex he's building, but I'm worried he's avoiding me. He's been super involved with the project until now and for him to miss three meetings in a row is just not like him."

Hopefully, he really *was* just busy. Considering how hands-on of a partner he was, she didn't even want to think about what would happen if it turned out they couldn't work with each other.

"And you're sure you don't just like him because he's keeping the tearoom?"

"I wouldn't be missing him so much if I were." Though she knew she'd made the right decision to not pursue a more intimate relationship, she'd often thought about their kiss and what would've happened if she hadn't stopped him.

"Then I think you should go for it," Stacy said.

Olivia propped her chin on her hand. "Now, how did I know you were going to say that?"

"Because you know I'm right," Stacy said, smiling, then shrugged. "I mean—what do you have to lose? It's not like things could get any worse. In fact, it might help to get rid of all the tension between you two. You wouldn't spend so much time thinking about what ifs and you could just get on with the project."

It was a tempting thought. Too tempting.

And hadn't she been thinking along the same lines these past few weeks? "I'm already paying the price," she murmured. Even if she didn't sleep with him, there'd still be a chance she'd be replaced on the project.

"Exactly!" Stacy's voice softened as she continued, "I know it would look bad—getting involved with a client—but it's not like you make a habit of it. If things don't work out, they don't. I doubt your dad would judge you for it—especially since he's always asking for grandchildren."

The mention of her dad made her frown. "There's nothing concrete yet, but my Yosemite hotel is hanging on the success of this project." And that would be her ticket out of franchisee management.

The fact that Dad had not only given her more responsibilities with The Mansion project, but was also considering her Yosemite proposal humbled her. She'd messed up so much with the Whitcombe and he still trusted her. She couldn't let him down.

"Then don't fail. And I know you won't, because it's The Mansion. No matter what happens between you and Adam, you'd never let it get between you and the hotel." Stacy made it sound so simple. "Besides, I've never heard you speak of anyone like you did just now about Adam. When's the last time you were this attracted to someone?"

"Never," Olivia answered honestly. There were times he was all she could think about. It was like she was back in the third grade with her first crush—Josh Hicks—except ten times worse because her desires weren't so innocent now. "And because of that, I know there's a chance of me falling for Adam. Big time." Instinctively, she knew that he had the power to hurt her.

"Would that be so bad?"

"It would if he didn't feel the same way and I have a feeling he's more the love 'em and leave 'em type." Sure, he'd made her feel special when they were together, but she sensed he had that effect on all women.

And though he probably didn't make it a habit to mix business with pleasure, she wasn't sure he felt as strongly as she did. She frowned. It didn't matter if he did or didn't. He was a client and getting involved with him was the height of unprofessionalism.

"And the shortest relationship you've ever been in was just shy of two years."

A beat passed and Olivia said, "You still think I should go for it, don't you?"

Stacy sighed. "Well, I've really only liked one guy, and I

guess I just feel that if I'd ever gotten the chance to be with him, for however long, I would've taken it in a heartbeat."

Olivia's chest tightened at the knowledge that Stacy was talking about her former bodyguard. It had probably been three years since he'd left, and her friend was still nursing a broken heart.

"Have you spoken with Brad lately?"

Stacy shook her head.

"You know my offer still stands. If you want me to hire him for an event or something so you can just happen to run into him, I will." Stacy deserved closure, at the very least. Brad hadn't even bothered to say goodbye.

"I appreciate it, but if he doesn't want to talk to me, then I don't want to talk with him either." She was quiet for a moment before continuing, "Besides, I am trying to move on. I go out and meet people."

"You go to parties and ask people for money," Olivia said dryly. Sometimes, she wondered if her friend asked for donations as a way to keep people away. Not a lot of people would be willing to get close to you when one of the first things you asked upon meeting them was for a donation.

Stacy laughed. "Hey—it's killing two birds with one stone."

Since she knew it was a hard topic for Stacy to talk about, Olivia changed subjects. "So, how's the gala coming along? Have you booked a caterer yet?"

Stacy took the bait and began talking about the menu she'd chosen.

But as Stacy talked about canapés, Olivia thought about her friend's situation with Brad and knew she didn't want to end up in the same boat. Years from now, would she look back and think about what would've happened if she'd taken a chance with Adam?

Probably, and she realized she didn't want to have any regrets.

# CHAPTER TEN

Olivia's stomach dropped as she walked into the meeting room and saw Adam's team, once again, without Adam. Considering that he hadn't been to a meeting in almost a month, she should've been used to his absence, but she was still disappointed.

Forcing a smile, she exchanged pleasantries before taking a seat. As the guys resumed their discussion about the upcoming baseball season, Olivia decided that Adam's absence was a good thing. There'd be no awkwardness if he skipped the meetings completely and he'd have no cause to remove her from the project. It was the perfect solution and yet she wasn't happy. It was almost as if she would rather spend time with him and risk getting kicked off, which was insane. She was so lost in thought she didn't notice the fact that Seth had entered the room until she heard the sound of the chair next to hers being rolled back.

"I think I have something you might like," the architect

said conspiratorially as he sat down. Her interest piqued, she watched as he removed a folder from his briefcase.

He handed her a rendering and she was surprised to see that it was a new concept for the lobby. He'd integrated some aspects of The Mansion's current design, like the ceiling finishing and the marble balustrade overlooking the main floor, with the more open, streamlined spaces of his initial design. And surprisingly, it worked really well. She'd been against removing the fresco in the check-in area but could now see that doing so would highlight the beautiful craftsmanship in the ceiling's woodwork.

"I love it," she said and suddenly realized that her grandfather's original design, while beautiful, had too many elements that had ended up clashing. This simpler design was classier and still maintained the beauty and elegance of the lobby. "Wow. Thank you so much for doing this. I really appreciate it." No one would've expected it of him—especially after they'd already approved his previous designs for the lobby.

"It's nothing," Seth said. "Since we're basically restoring the ballroom and the tearoom, I wanted a more cohesive design throughout the hotel to create a more harmonious flow."

Hope bloomed inside her at the thought of keeping more of her grandfather's design intact before reality settled in. Adam still needed to approve the design. She handed the rendering to Ricky. "Do you think Adam will like it?"

"I'll ask him." Ricky took a moment to look at the new design, then glanced at Seth.

Seth nodded. "I'll email you a copy."

"How did you learn to do stuff like this?" Olivia couldn't help but ask. He always found ways to make small but meaningful changes.

"I was lucky enough to work for Tom Fielding," he said, referring to the famous postmodern architect, then laughed. "Well. I didn't think so at the time. It felt like a lot of busy work. He would hand-draw everything and we would then have to convert everything to CAD. But at the end of the day, it was the best training I could've ever had. I learned a lot about design from breaking things down and putting them back together. Hey, I forgot you studied architecture. Where did you intern?"

Olivia's cheeks warmed. "I didn't. I dropped out right after my third year to help out here."

Sometimes, she still felt as if she'd taken the easy way out. She'd always loved design and had constantly been drawing buildings as a child. But she'd really struggled in college, more so than any of her classmates, it had seemed. She'd work for weeks on a project only for it to be torn apart in Studio.

The criticism had been valid, but she'd always had a hard time integrating the feedback. She'd fix a problem, but in the process, somehow create a bigger problem than the original one. And that had been when the professor had actually told her what was wrong.

There'd been times a professor or critic would call her work uninspired or pedestrian, then expect her to improve upon it. More often than not, she'd ended up redoing the assignment with a completely different idea, because she hadn't even known how to start addressing the problem.

"And let me guess, you were relieved when you left?"

Olivia laughed. "I was," she admitted. "No matter how hard I tried, I never got a hang of manipulating light and textures conceptually. It seemed as if every semester, I was praying for the professors to shift to a more tangible approach. I did pretty well when it came to real sites and actual structures, but was constantly hanging by a thread with everything else."

"And most everything at school is abstract," he said, and she nodded.

"Exactly."

He sighed. "You know, I personally struggled with adapting 3D models to paper the whole time I was at school. I knew what I wanted in my head. I just couldn't convey it properly on a 2D scale."

She blinked in surprise. She hadn't expected someone of his caliber to have struggled with such a fundamental part of architecture. He'd probably had as hard a time as her, but instead of dropping out, he'd pushed through and had become an amazing architect.

It was a humbling thought.

"But let me tell you," he continued. "Interning with Fielding taught me more about bringing my visions to life than Studio ever did. I won't lie and say that it gets better. Just a little less than half of the people in my undergrad class actually graduated. But the work afterwards was nothing like school. Everything is based on real working sites. So you should definitely take another look at architecture if you're interested in that side of things."

She'd heard the same, but a part of her worried that she simply didn't have what it takes to graduate. Though she'd passed all her classes, there'd been times she almost hadn't. And for someone who'd almost always gotten straight A's, it had been disheartening to work so hard in school and yet barely pass.

"And if you ever decide to go back to school, you can intern at my firm."

"Thanks. I really appreciate it." Due to a conflict of interest, she'd never take him up on the offer, but she was touched that he'd made it.

"Of course. You have a good knack for design, which I —" He stopped as the door opened and Tina walked in, along with the rest of Montgomery's team. He shot her an apologetic look before he grabbed his things and took his place in the front of the room.

Once everyone was seated, he started his presentation.

As Seth talked about his vision for the hotel shops, Olivia looked at his new design for the lobby and was, once again, amazed by how the simplest of changes could bring out the elegance of the room.

Wishing she could do the same, she found herself thinking about ways she could go back to school. Perhaps she could enroll in a few classes so that she wouldn't be too stressed or maybe she could retake some of her old classes and see how she fared.

Surely, it would be easier the second time around…

* * *

"Hey, Adam. Thanks for seeing me on such short notice," Edward Monroe said as he walked into Adam's office.

"You know my door's always open for you," he told the investigator. "What did you find?"

He already knew his parents had started the rumors about him, but he wanted to know exactly how far-reaching these rumors actually were. Were there other companies who'd wanted to rent spaces from him, but had decided not to like Landon's?

He couldn't imagine there'd be many people who'd take the time to vet the rumors the way Jake had. In fact, most companies would've probably taken the rumors at face value and moved on, costing him untold amounts of business.

And since his parents were incapable of listening to reason, he'd fight fire with fire. A part of him hated that he was stooping to their level. He'd always taken the high road when it came to them and had never engaged whenever they were looking for a fight. But they were coming after his business now and he wouldn't take that sitting down.

He wouldn't make up rumors as they'd done with him, but he could certainly air their dirty laundry for all to see.

Edward sighed. "I'm afraid you aren't going to like it. It looks like it was your brother who started the rumors—not your parents."

Adam stared dumbstruck at the man. Sure, he and Doug

weren't exactly close, but his brother would never do that to him.

"There must be some mistake," Adam finally said when he found his voice. Not only was Doug a good person, but he also knew what it was like to be ganged up on by their parents. He wouldn't help them hurt Adam.

*Although they did keep Doug on payroll even though he didn't do a damn thing…*

"I'm sorry," Edward said. "I confirmed it with two separate sources."

Adam shook his head and thought about the last time he'd seen Doug. It had been last month, when the three siblings had gotten together for dinner. There'd been absolutely nothing about Doug's behavior that would've been cause for concern. Doug had been just as fun and easygoing as ever.

There was no way he could be behind the attacks, but maybe he knew something about the rumors. Perhaps an acquaintance of his had maligned AC Developments and when Doug hadn't corrected the person, people assumed it was true?

It was a stretch, but it was more believable than his brother sabotaging him. He'd call Doug once Edward was gone to see what he knew. Then hopefully, Adam could point Edward in the right direction.

As Edward summarized the conversations he'd had, Adam couldn't help noting that they were all second-hand accounts. None of the people had spoken with Doug directly and Adam took heart in that. There had to be some kind of misunderstanding.

After Edward left, Adam grabbed his cell phone and called his brother. Doug answered after a few rings.

"Hey, Adam. What's up?"

"Are you telling people that I'm financially insolvent?" he asked and inwardly winced. He'd been planning on easing into the conversation, but these rumors were turning him inside out.

"No. Of course not! Wait—maybe I did."

A sense of foreboding filled Adam. "Explain."

"Well, there was this really cute girl and she thought I was you. I told her she was looking for the wrong Campbell brother and may have implied that you were cash-strapped."

Adam groaned. "And let me guess, this was at a party?" Though his brother wasn't motivated to do anything more than have a good time, he had a lot of friends who were well connected. Out of the three siblings, Doug was the only one who'd taken their parents' mantra of "it's who you know" to heart.

"Yeah. At Alan Plummer's birthday party." So, that would explain why the rumors were so widespread. Plummer was the CEO of Teller's Bank. With his luck, the woman Doug had been trying to impress was some hot shot banker as well. Or perhaps, someone else had over-heard. "Why? Did something happen?" Doug asked, and Adam shook his head. Would his brother ever learn that there were consequences to his actions?

"Landon's—the restaurant chain—pulled out of the Plex because they heard rumors that I was insolvent. The permits had already been approved and we were just about to start construction."

"Aww, shit. I'm really sorry, Adam. Do you want me to say anything?"

"No. That would just make things worse. Look, I would really appreciate it if you didn't talk about me or my financial situation in the future." Hopefully, the rumors would die down on their own when people saw that he was doing okay. It helped that it was just a one-time thing and not the constant attack he'd thought his parents were orchestrating.

"I'm sorry."

Adam sighed. Though he was disappointed with Doug, he also knew that his brother's brain went haywire whenever he saw a beautiful woman. "I hope you got the girl's number?"

"We went on a few dates, but it didn't work out."

Of course it didn't.

Adam guessed it wasn't too surprising that he and his siblings never had serious relationships. What sane person would after witnessing their parents' marriage? He knew his parents must've been in love once. His father wouldn't have married someone who wasn't rich or powerful otherwise. But somehow, their love had twisted into some sick version of it where it seemed both their goals were to hurt the other with their affairs. They loved making each other miserable and would've divorced years ago if they weren't so concerned about appearances and money.

Martha liked to think it was their mom's controlling ways that had caused Dad to seek affairs. Since Mom hadn't been born into money the way Dad had, she overcompensated by making sure the family was never seen lacking. They always had to wear the right clothes, act a certain way, and be seen at the most exclusive events. But since Dad was the same way, Adam doubted that was the reason.

Considering how awful Mom and Dad were, it was more believable that they would've made whomever they married miserable. It was just Adam's and his siblings' luck that the two had found each other and had them.

Knowing that he and his siblings were luckier than most people, Adam sighed. He should just be happy that he wasn't under their control anymore.

Once he and Doug disconnected, the realization that his parents had nothing to do with the rumors struck, surprising him. He couldn't believe it. They were innocent. But why then had his father called the other week? Was it possible he'd just wanted to say hi?

Guilt assailed him at the way he'd reacted and he considered calling his dad to apologize before he crossed the thought off. Just because his father hadn't started the rumors didn't mean he wasn't up to no good.

Because frankly, Dad *never* called unless he wanted something.

Still, it felt good to know that his parents hadn't spread the rumors, and Adam made a mental note to be more cordial the next time he spoke to either of them.

# CHAPTER ELEVEN

As she waited for an elevator, Olivia mentally reviewed her talking points for her upcoming meeting with Julian Spa.

Montgomery usually ran their own spas inside their hotels, but she wanted to move away from that business model. They were one of the top brands in luxury hotels, but they were nowhere near the best in spas. And it just didn't make sense to compete with the best when they could simply ask one of them to open a spa in their hotels.

Julian Spa would get a steep discount in rent, Montgomery would get more sales, and their customers would know they were getting the best of the best. Her dad and Adam had okayed the plan and if they got a deal, The Mansion would be their first hotel to feature another company's spa.

The elevator doors opened, and she was surprised to see Adam step out. It was the first time she'd seen him since he'd brought her cake, and she had to stop herself from grinning like a fool. She'd missed him.

It was ridiculous.

They'd agreed to make their working relationship a priority, yet here she was, drinking in the sight of him as if he might suddenly disappear again. With those broad shoulders of his filling out his dark suit, he looked better than she remembered, and she suddenly realized how much trouble she was in.

It was much easier to tell herself to keep things on a professional level when he wasn't standing right in front of her. Because no matter how tempted she was to throw caution to the wind, she couldn't risk her position on The Mansion and her dreams to build a small chain of hotels for a man.

Their eyes locked and his gaze warmed. She liked to think he was happy to see her, too, but she knew it was just wishful thinking. His gaze lowered to her briefcase and he stretched out an arm to stop the elevator. "Going down?" She nodded, and he said, "I'll ride with you."

"Did you want to speak with me?" she asked as she stepped in.

"Yeah. I wanted to talk about The Mansion." Concern filled her as to what he might want to discuss, but she didn't want to be late.

"I'm actually on my way to a meeting with Julian Spa."

"Why don't I go with you and we can talk on the way?"

His offer to accompany her caught her off guard, but it shouldn't have. Even when he didn't go to the meetings, he was still more active in the decision-making process than any of the other clients she'd worked with. He'd even approved of Seth's changes of the lobby just hours after the meeting. After dealing with franchisees who sometimes took weeks to respond, it was a nice change of pace.

"All right."

The fact that he was tagging along eased her worries. She doubted he'd go if he were dissatisfied with her performance. And while she was pleased at the thought of spending time with him, a part of her wondered if he was testing the waters to see whether or not they could work together. If he was, she'd show him that not only was she capable of keeping things professional, but that she was also capable of negotiating a good deal for The Mansion.

"Is this the company you mentioned that has a spa near the hotel?" he asked.

"Yeah," she said, pleased that he remembered such a small detail. "They have one two blocks away." Another option was Summerville, but she preferred Julian because the company's positioning and values suited the Montgomery brand more. It was high class and yet approachable, while Summerville, though unparalleled in its customer service, could be intimidating at times.

She lifted her handbag. "I brought the numbers. Most of the people who use Montgomery Spas are guests and I believe the numbers are sufficient enough to justify opening up another location without cannibalizing their existing sales. Thanks for allowing me to pursue this, by the way." She'd wanted to do something similar with their Los Angeles hotel, but the franchisee hadn't wanted to reduce the hotel's earnings in any way.

"It's nothing. I'm thinking the Julian brand will entice the guests who wouldn't ordinarily have gone to the spa to do so and that the extra business will more than make up for the reduced profit margins."

She thought so too and was grateful that Adam was turning out to be such an agreeable partner.

* * *

"And you would take care of all the sheets, towels, and such?" Greg Mateik, Julian's VP of operations, asked an hour and a half later.

Olivia gritted her teeth. She'd answered that particular question twice now. "Yes, we'd take care of all of that," she repeated, and before he asked again, she added, "as well as all the utensils and dishes," referring to the plates and cups Julian used when they offered tea and biscuits to their customers.

She began to fear she'd made a mistake in approaching Julian. She knew Greg was the son-in-law of the owner, but she couldn't believe that they'd allow someone who was so hard to talk with become VP of operations. Not only that, he was nickel and diming everything and she couldn't help but be reminded of Don Frazer, a franchisee who questioned almost every line item on their statements.

She dreaded the hours-long call from him every quarter and unfortunately, he never missed a single one. There was nothing she could do about Don since he was a long-time client, but she wouldn't willingly go into business with someone like him if she could prevent it. Besides, how much could washing some sheets cost anyway? It didn't seem like something that could make or break a deal.

"And what about our products?"

Olivia frowned. "What do you mean?"

"Would Montgomery also get a share of our product sales?"

Her hand clenched beneath the table. She couldn't believe he had the nerve to ask her that after she'd already told him that Montgomery would advertise the products in the lobby and in their catalog.

Doing her best to keep her voice even, she answered, "If the customer buys them at the hotel, then yes. We would get the same percentage as the spa services."

She could just imagine how he'd push her on everything if they partnered up. And while she agreed that it was good to get certain details hammered out before they delved further into discussions, this was too much. She simply didn't want to do business with someone like Greg.

Her cheeks warmed at the thought of how incompetent she must look to Adam right now. First, she'd highlighted all her failures over dinner and now this! He was no doubt regretting his decision to keep her on and was probably wondering if it was too late to have her replaced or not.

"That doesn't seem fair. The products wouldn't even take up that much space."

"And you want us to cover the credit card fees for those, too?" she asked, referring to their earlier talks, where he'd wanted to get paid based on total revenues instead of net receivables.

"Well—we could have two credit card machines," he said, and she inwardly groaned. This was getting ridiculous. She had the brief notion of going above Greg to talk to someone else at Julian before she quickly crossed off the idea. Not only would the business relationship start off on the wrong foot, but the higher-ups could always delegate the task to Greg, and she'd be stuck dealing with him again.

It was too bad, because Julian would've been a great fit for Montgomery.

Her cell phone's screen lit up. She would've normally ignored it, but they were just wasting time here. There was no way she would do business with them. She picked up her phone and saw that it was a text from Adam.

*SOS?*

Glad for an excuse to get out of the meeting, she resisted the urge to smile at Adam. She'd thank him later. "I'm sorry, Greg. I'm afraid we have to go. Something's come up at the office."

"Okay. I'll send you an email with my other questions."

"Great," she said as she stood. She made sure she had everything and said, "It was nice meeting you."

"Yes, you, too," he said as he shook her hand, then Adam's. "I look forward to working with you and Montgomery."

She couldn't get out of the office fast enough, but she made certain to measure her pace as they walked through the lobby. She'd review Summerville's offerings as soon as she got to the office. After the awful meeting Adam had just witnessed, she was eager to set things right and find a replacement as quickly as she could.

"So, that was a total bust," Adam said once they left the office suite.

"I'm sorry for wasting your time and thanks so much

for the save." She liked that he'd given her a choice by sending her a text. Considering how bad the meeting had gone, he could've easily pretended to get a text himself and cut the meeting short, but he'd thrown the ball in her court, and she appreciated that.

"It wasn't a complete bust. Those cookies were delicious," he said, and she laughed.

They reached the elevators and he pressed the down button. As they waited, a man in a suit walked by and slowly looked her over from head to toe, before giving her a smile.

From behind her, she felt Adam take a protective step towards her. The man's eyes turned cold as he gave a hard nod before continuing on his way.

She inwardly groaned. She already liked Adam more than was wise. But with how he'd acted today—letting her decide if she wanted to end the meeting and now this—she was falling hard and fast. She had no defenses against someone who was not only sexy as sin, but considerate too.

"Thanks for having my back," she murmured as the elevator doors opened and they walked in. But in the back of her mind, she couldn't help worrying about her growing feelings for him and how they would affect their working relationship.

Olivia thought he'd been trying to protect her.

It was probably better to let her continue thinking that instead of the real reason. He'd seen the man look at her and had wanted to stake his territory. Wanting to show her that it wasn't because of any kindness that he'd done that, he pulled her towards him and kissed her. She stilled and he belatedly remembered that she hadn't wanted that guy's attention and had already rebuffed his own advances.

He released her. "I shouldn't have—" He was cut off when she pulled his head down for another kiss.

Wrapping his arms around her, he deepened the kiss. Sweet. She tasted so damn sweet. He wanted more. Nibbling her lips, he coaxed them apart. She moaned as his tongue slid against hers, and the sound went straight to his cock.

The elevator dinged and they pulled apart as the doors opened. Pride filled him when her eyes opened, and he saw her dazed look. He'd done that to her. He wanted to do even more things to her but knew she needed time to think before she made any decisions.

Two people entered the elevator before the doors closed again. The silence was deafening, and he was caught off guard by how much he wanted to feel her in his arms again. She'd felt so perfect—as if she belonged there.

It seemed like forever when the elevator finally stopped at the lobby. "So, I guess you have some extra time since the meeting was cut short?" he asked as they walked towards the door.

Though his voice was calm, he was a mess inside. His heart was racing, and it took all that he had not to grab hold of her again.

She nodded, and he continued, "My office is a few blocks from here. Do you want to see the new complex I'm building?" While he'd much rather take her to his place, he was surprised to find that he wanted to spend time with her in any way possible. What's more, he actually wanted to show her the project that was coming to mean so much to him.

"I'd love to," she said, and a warmth spread through him at the thought of her wanting to know more about him and what he did.

# CHAPTER TWELVE

Olivia looked at the model of the Plex, the outdoor shopping complex Adam was building, impressed. It was a lot nicer than what she'd been expecting. With the way Adam had described it, she'd been expecting something more along the lines of a strip mall, but this was a full-on complex, complete with a movie theater, restaurants, shops, and even a hotel. A Stone House hotel.

"Why didn't you use Stone House for The Mansion?" she asked, curious.

Stone House had a good reputation and had a high-end division Montgomery competed with. She thought Montgomery was the better brand, but also knew she was too biased to make an impartial decision.

"Stone House has been a really great partner for us, but I wanted something better for The Mansion."

"And for The Mansion to be more than just one of their many locations in New York," she said, and he nodded.

Though it didn't lessen her guilt, she suddenly realized

that losing the Whitcombe might've been a good thing. If they hadn't, Adam might've never approached them about The Mansion.

And while she'd wanted The Mansion back under the Montgomery umbrella for as long as she could remember, it was Adam she was thinking of right now. Hell. He'd been all she could think about for weeks. First, with their kiss after dinner together and now the kiss in the elevator.

She was still surprised by her brazenness to kiss him after he'd pulled away, but some part of her had known that he wouldn't kiss her again, and the thought had been unbearable.

So she'd kissed him for all that she was worth and he'd responded in kind.

Shivers coursed through her as she remembered it. She didn't think she'd ever gotten so turned on from just a kiss and could just imagine how amazing sex with him would be. Their embrace in the elevator had been so thrilling and hot and the fact that he hadn't pressured her made her want him even more.

It would be foolish to sleep with him, but she didn't want to listen to reason. Realizing that she was staring at the lips that had kissed her so thoroughly, she looked down at the model, her cheeks flushing.

"Where exactly is this?" she asked as she forced herself to concentrate on the conversation. He'd seemed so proud to show her his work. The least she could do was pay attention.

"It's about thirty minutes outside of Houston—in Clear Lake."

"Where the space center is?"

He nodded. "And a lot of businesses."

"So, you'll get both tourists and business travelers." Montgomery often looked for the same thing except in bigger cities, though her Yosemite hotel wouldn't be like that. Since the hotel wouldn't be close to any corporate headquarters, they'd have to rely mainly on tourists. Although she *could* see businesses interested in hosting retreats and conferences there…

"That's what we're hoping."

Something in his tone made her look up and she was surprised to find him watching her lips. His gaze rose to meet hers and a delicious thrill shot through her at the heat she saw there. She couldn't help but love the fact that he liked her for her. So many times, men had pretended interest in her to get access to one of her family members, but Adam wasn't like that. He already had his business deal, and all the terms were set.

Which meant that he'd kissed her because he'd wanted to.

Not only that, he'd even gotten jealous over her. She didn't think she'd ever made anyone jealous and the thought was heady. She'd worried that he might not return her feelings, but what if he did?

"Let's go to my place?"

Nerves wrecked her the moment the words were out of her mouth. She'd never done anything like this before, then again, no one had ever made her feel this way either. And she found herself wanting to do something for herself. She'd worry about the consequences later.

A beat passed before he nodded. "I'll drive."

* * *

Adam's heart sped as he practically ran up the steps of Olivia's brownstone. He knew this was a bad idea, but he couldn't find the strength to put a stop to things. He didn't want to.

She'd been all he could think about for weeks. Even when he'd poured himself into work, hoping to forget her, she'd still wormed her way into his thoughts at night.

Her movements were sure and precise as she opened the door and he wished he could be as calm. He wanted to take things slow and to savor every moment, but after wanting her for so long, he was just too pumped.

As soon as they were inside and the door was closed, he pinned her to it and kissed her. Her hands greedily roamed his chest, sending shivers coursing through him, as she peppered kisses on his chin, then throat. She removed his suit jacket, then started unbuttoning his shirt.

He reached for her dress's zipper and felt his throat dry when the dress gaped open to reveal her lace-covered breasts. He immediately wrapped his mouth over one and bit it gently. Gasping, she wrapped an arm around him, pulling him closer.

Smiling, he laved the nipple and felt his head grow dizzy with the sounds she was making. As he moved to give attention to her other breast, she reached for his belt. She brushed against his hardness and his whole body went haywire. Worried that he'd mess up before they'd started, he pulled away.

"I'll do my pants and you—" His gaze dropped to her matching lace panties. He'd taste her later, he promised himself.

Thankfully, she understood what he wanted and removed the panties. The small triangular patch tantalized him, and he momentarily forgot what he was supposed to be doing. She took a step towards him and he remembered. He quickly removed his pants and got a condom.

He touched her folds and was grateful to find her moist and slick. He slipped a finger into her and groaned. Damn. She was tight. Her eyes fluttered as her head fell back on a moan. Loving how responsive she was, he inserted another finger. After a few pumps, he couldn't wait any longer. He removed his hand and quickly donned the condom.

He grabbed her hips, lifting her, and drove into her. His eyes rolled to the back of his head as her hot sheath engulfed him. She felt so good. As if they'd done it a million times, they moved in perfect harmony.

Her legs wrapped around him, pushing him even deeper inside of her. He dragged her bra down, unveiling her luscious breasts, and began sucking on one.

Her nails digging into his back, she cried out as she began to spasm. The sensation of her squeezing around him sent him flying over the edge and they came together. Her legs weakened and he tightened his hold on her before resting his forehead on hers.

Damn. He'd known they'd be good together, but he hadn't been expecting that. Already wanting her again, he lowered his mouth to hers, taking his time as he tasted every inch of her.

"So that was something," she said when they parted, and he laughed.

"Yeah. Yeah, it was." He felt as if he'd just run through Central Park and he really wanted to do so again. But this time, he wanted to take things slow and explore more of that delicious body of hers.

She was so sensitive. He could already imagine the sounds she'd make when he found a particularly sensitive spot. He grinned as he lifted her away from the door. "Bedroom, now."

* * *

"So, what made you change your mind about us?" Adam asked as they lay curled in bed hours later. "Not that I'm complaining, of course."

"I guess I just wanted to do something for myself for a change." She'd probably regret the decision in the morning, but for now, she was content to lay in his arms and savor the moment.

"So, I'm a treat to yourself."

She laughed as she turned towards him. Considering she'd just had the best sex of her life, it was an apt description. But it hadn't just been great sex. There'd been a real connection, too. She'd never felt so in sync with someone before and hoped he felt the same.

"You are. I guess I've always been conscious of how my

actions reflect on my family and just once, I wanted to throw caution to the wind."

"You're really close to your family, aren't you?"

"I am. Perhaps it's because we worked together at the hotel for so many years, but we've always been close." She hadn't realized it then, but she really hit the jackpot with her parents. While other parents left the rearing of their children to nannies or daycare, her parents had basically been on top of her and her brother practically twenty-four seven. Yes, they'd been overbearing at times, but she and Robbie had always known that their parents would be there for them. "How about you? I know you aren't close to your parents, but how about your siblings?"

"I'm really close to my sister, Martha. We were only a grade apart at school, so we were always tight. Doug, on the other hand, is seven years younger than me. By the time he was in the first grade, I was already going to my grandfather's factory after school. We get along fine, but I'm not sure if we would've even kept in touch if it weren't for Martha always inviting us to meet up."

There was a pause before he spoke again. "My dad paid off my dream school to reject me." She stilled, and he continued, "I wanted to study chemistry to work on the technical side of the business while my dad wanted me to study business at his alma mater. I made a deal with my parents that if I maintained a three-point-eight GPA and was accepted into my dream school, they'd allow me to study chemistry." He shook his head. "I don't think they ever expected me to make it. I'd never been much of a student, but I studied really hard and got in. But they had other plans."

"That's horrible!"

He shrugged. "At least, I know what he did. If it wasn't for the family's lawyer accidentally cc'ing me on the dean's thank-you letter to my dad, I would've never found out. Hell. I wouldn't have even believed it." He laughed bitterly. "I'd actually been looking forward to working with my dad and putting my plans for the company into motion."

"Have you spoken with your parents since?"

"I usually see them once a year at my sister's birthday party, but I actually just talked to my dad last month."

"Was he trying to make amends?"

She hated the thought of him not getting along with his parents. What they'd done to him was unthinkable, but she doubted there'd been any ill intent. They'd probably just been trying to do what they thought was right. But parents were human and made mistakes, too.

"He said he wanted to meet for dinner sometime, which is crazy, because he and Mom can barely stand the sight of me. I asked if either of them was sick, but he said they were fine."

"Are you going to see them?"

"We haven't made plans, but I think I will if either one of them calls again."

Thinking that perhaps all he needed was a little push to reconcile with his parents, she wondered if there was anything she could do and suddenly remembered that Dannier had a spa.

Maybe a business deal could be the first step to healing

the rift between Adam and his parents. Dannier's spa wasn't as established as Julian or Summerville, but their brand was certainly more recognizable to the average American. Their facial cream was sold in practically every department store and had an almost cult-like following.

She'd look into it tomorrow before running the idea by Adam. But the more she thought about it, the more she liked the idea of integrating Adam's family's business with hers. And a small part of her wondered if the reason Greg Mateik had been such a nitpick was because Julian was so successful. Perhaps they fielded offers so often they could afford to be as demanding as they wanted. Dannier, on the other hand, was still starting out as a spa and would probably be hungrier for business opportunities.

Speaking of hunger, she suddenly realized the time. "Did you want to order something to eat?"

"Are you hungry?"

"No."

Mischief filled his eyes as he ran a hand down her arm. "Then I can think of better ways to spend our time," he said, then proceeded to prove his point.

# CHAPTER THIRTEEN

A movement awakened Adam the next morning. He looked to his side and saw that Olivia had curled her body into his in her sleep. A smile tugged at his lips as the events from yesterday flashed through his head—of him taking her against the door, of her sucking him off as she gazed up at him with those beautiful brown eyes, of them eating Thai in bed… It was definitely something he could get used to.

The thought surprised him. He *never* spent the night with the women he had sex with. Not only did he not want the women to get the idea that he was interested in more than a one-night stand, but there always came a time when the urge to leave overwhelmed him. But for some reason, that feeling hadn't shown up yesterday. Hell. It hadn't even come this morning.

He should've known he'd feel differently about Olivia.

He never mixed business with pleasure. In fact, whenever he'd felt an attraction to a woman with whom he had a working relationship, he simply told himself to move on, and he did. But he just hadn't been able to do that with Olivia. She'd gotten under his skin and wouldn't leave.

She'd had reservations about them getting involved due to their business relationship, but hopefully this wasn't just a one-night stand for her. Because he was nowhere near getting his fill of her.

Damn. He'd already had trouble being in the same room with her. Now that he knew how his name sounded on her lips as she came, the feel of her in his arms, he didn't know how he'd survive another meeting if he couldn't look forward to spending more nights with her. The whole meeting, he'd just think about what he was missing.

As if sensing that she was cuddling him, she opened her eyes and looked up. She was so beautiful he couldn't stop himself from bending his head to kiss her.

"I want to see you again," he said when they broke apart.

"We have a meeting with Prism on Friday," she said, referring to The Mansion's current operator, and he groaned. *Please say that she was kidding.* A sexy smile curved her lips as she grabbed his butt and squeezed. "I'm free tonight."

"Now that's more like it." A weight he hadn't known was there suddenly lifted off him. He bent down to kiss her again when she looked at something behind him, her eyes widening.

"Oh," she said as she jumped out of bed. Curious, he turned around and saw a clock. He didn't know if he should laugh or be insulted.

"I'm sorry," she said as she opened her closet and

grabbed a blouse. "I'm usually on the way to work right now." That was another thing he liked about her. Like him, she was born into money, but she wasn't using that as an excuse to not work.

She leaned over to open a drawer and he forgot how to think as he looked at that perfectly shaped butt. She got a bra and underwear and he suddenly remembered himself. This was her place and he still had to drive her to her office, where they'd left her car.

He got out of bed to look for his clothes, but in the back of his mind, he was already counting the hours until he could take off those panties she'd just grabbed.

* * *

"Would you mind if we don't advertise the fact that we're together in the office?" Olivia asked Adam while they were lying in bed together that night. They'd intended to go out to dinner, but after she'd walked into his apartment and kissed him, he'd been a goner.

"Why? Are you embarrassed about me?" he teased.

"Of course not, but I know how bad this looks. I mean, I could just imagine how I'd feel if one of our employees slept with a client. I don't mind other people knowing, but I don't want anyone in the office thinking differently about us or afraid to say anything critical."

"No. I definitely understand." He wouldn't be happy if an employee of his started dating one of their business partners either. "So basically, no butt grabbing or stealing kisses in the hallway?"

A smile tugged at her lips. "Yeah."

"So, I guess I have to make up for the lost time, huh?" he said before he kissed her. Her soft lips yielded to him and he deepened the kiss, exploring her mouth, and getting drunk on her sweetness.

After a while, she put her hand on him and pushed him away. "Wait. There's another thing I wanted to ask you." His eyebrows rose and she groaned. "I can't think with your naked chest right there." He grinned at the knowledge that he affected her. It felt good to know that he wasn't the only one feeling this way.

She hadn't removed her hand from him either. In fact, she was currently stroking his chest. Sighing, he moved to his side of the bed. Unfortunately, she pulled the bedsheet up to cover her breasts.

"How would you feel about using Dannier as our spa in The Mansion? They only have a few spas—"

He was still looking at that damn sheet that was covering her breasts, so it took a moment for her words to register and when it did, his good mood evaporated.

"Absolutely not," he said, interrupting her.

Olivia froze, then started hesitantly, "It's not like we're giving Dannier any special treatment. Though they're new in the industry, they've been steadily gaining market share. Along with their brand recognition—"

"I don't care if they're the number one spa in the world, we're not having them in The Mansion." In fact, having a Dannier spa in the hotel would defeat the purpose of rubbing his success in his parents' faces.

How could Olivia even ask that of him?

She knew how he felt about his parents. Remembering how close she was to her family, he narrowed his eyes. "Are you trying to patch things up between me and my parents?"

She looked like she was about to deny it before she sighed. "A little, I guess. I do think we'd do well with Dannier, but I also thought it would be easier for you guys to make amends if you had a business relationship first."

He groaned as he ran a hand down his face.

He should've known she'd try to "help." But there was no repairing his relationship with his parents. That option had vanished long ago. And while he was frustrated that she'd try to butt into his affairs, a part of him liked that she cared enough about him to try, but he had to draw the line.

"Let's get one thing straight," he said as he sat up. "If we're going to continue seeing each other, you will not try to fix my relationship, or lack thereof, with my parents."

"I understand. I won't do it again," she said solemnly, and he hated the thought of her thinking badly of him. He knew how important family was to her, but his parents were just awful human beings.

"My parents are not good people," he started. The fact that they hadn't been the ones to spread rumors about him didn't take away from all the other horrible things they'd done. "They used me to screw over my widowed aunt and cousin."

He'd never told anyone the whole story before, but he needed her to understand how dangerous his parents were. "My grandpa had always planned to give equal portions of the company to his two sons but changed his mind when it became clear that my uncle—my dad's brother—was horrible with money. My uncle was a compulsive gambler and often lost everything only to win it back again. After my uncle died, my parents told my grandpa that they'd give my Aunt Helen and Cousin Louie an equal share of the profits if he left everything to my dad."

Adam's throat tightened at the memory of his grandpa asking him to promise that he'd take care of his aunt and cousin when he was in charge of Dannier. Not knowing what his parents were doing, Adam had thought it had been Grandpa's way of underlining how important family was and had readily agreed.

"Thinking that I would run Dannier after my father, my grandfather relented. Since I was his first grandchild, he'd always had a soft spot for me, which only grew when I became interested in Dannier. But after my grandpa died, my parents put a halt to the distributions and increased my dad's salary."

He was still ashamed to admit that he hadn't even known about it. He and his siblings had only found out about the perfidy after Martha had invited Aunt Helen and her son to her birthday party. Martha had been surprised when their usually friendly aunt had wanted nothing to do with them. Wanting answers, Martha had pushed Aunt Helen until she finally told her why she was so angry.

It had taken some time for Adam and his siblings to convince their aunt that they'd known nothing of their parents' plans, but she'd finally forgiven them.

He hated that he'd unwittingly helped his parents screw his aunt and cousin from their rightful inheritance. Though

Louie had a trust fund from their grandfather, it was nothing compared to what was rightfully his.

"Your poor aunt!"

"I tried to help her out after I started making money, but she had too much pride."

He sometimes wondered if there was anything he could've done to stop his parents. If he'd spent more time at home, perhaps he would've known what they were up to. Instead, he'd spent as much time as he could at the factory to avoid hearing his parents' constant yelling and fighting.

But he guessed he should be grateful that his parents were always fighting. It was scary to think about what they could accomplish when they joined forces and worked together.

He nodded at Olivia. "Please tell me you have another company in mind for the spa." She'd been so happy when she'd suggested Dannier. He hated the thought of letting her down.

"I was thinking about Summerville before I thought about Dannier, but I thought Dannier would be hungrier because they're still in the early stages of their spa business. I'll contact Summerville next week."

Suddenly realizing that Olivia was just the kind of woman his parents would want him to marry, he warned her. "If my parents ever try to contact you, you have my permission to tell them to fuck off."

Considering how they'd always wanted to be part of the old money crowd, it wasn't crazy to imagine that they'd see Olivia as their way in. They might even try to mend fences with him.

She laughed. "Hopefully, it won't come to that."

Adam couldn't help but wonder what Olivia must think of him. She was so close to her family and even worked with them while he didn't even want to see his. Hoping to distract her from their differences, he kissed her, then playfully smacked her butt.

"We better get going." Their reservation was already long gone, but he knew the restaurant would seat them regardless.

# CHAPTER FOURTEEN

Olivia sighed happily as she mentally replayed the events of yesterday's date with Adam. He'd taken her on a private tour of the zoo, where they'd gotten to pet and feed the animals.

She smiled as she remembered him feeding the bears. He'd tried to hide it, but he hadn't been comfortable, and she'd had to resist the urge to laugh. He'd done much better with the adorable red pandas.

"Olivia?"

"Hmmm?"

"Olivia! Will you please pass the butter?"

It took a second for Mom's words to register and when it did, Olivia winced. She grabbed the butter and handed it to her mom. "Sorry." The family met up for brunch every Sunday at the club and she guessed she was a little distracted today.

Mom smiled knowingly. "So, when will you be bringing Adam to brunch?"

She shouldn't be surprised her mom knew about her and Adam, but she was. Though they hadn't exactly kept their relationship a secret, they hadn't advertised the fact, either.

She guessed that meant Dad knew as well.

She briefly thought about apologizing for getting involved with a client before she crossed the thought off. He'd been interested in setting her up with Adam from the outset, so she doubted he'd put up a fight now. Besides, he was probably encouraged by the thought of her settling down than anything else.

But she'd only been seeing Adam for a month—definitely nowhere near the meet-the-parents stage, though perhaps things were different since Adam had already met Dad… No. That didn't seem right. He shouldn't feel obligated to come to brunch because of their working relationship. If he met her family, it should be because he wanted to, not because he felt forced to. Her family deserved better than that.

"I'm not ready for him to meet the family yet," she admitted. "It's just so new." She could already imagine her mom asking Adam what his intentions towards her daughter were and knew she couldn't put him through that.

And deep down, she was afraid of what his answer would be. Though it wasn't as if she were looking for a commitment, Adam had come to mean something to her and she didn't want to scare him off.

"Oh. We understand, but don't take too long, honey.

Tamara Blake already asked about him. She saw you two at Monsieur Augustin."

"Oh. I didn't see her." If she had, she would've called so that Mom wouldn't have found out from someone else.

Guilt filled her at what her mom must've thought when she'd gotten the call. They'd always been so close, but after hearing Mom's excitement after she'd mentioned having dinner with Adam that first time, she'd purposely kept Mom in the dark when she and Adam had started seeing each other.

On top of not wanting to get her mom's hopes up, she knew Mom would want to meet Adam. But considering how he felt about his parents, she doubted he wanted anything to do with hers.

"I'm sorry you had to find out that way."

"As long as Adam likes children, I'll forgive you."

"Mom!" Her brother snickered and she did her best not to make a face at him.

"Well. You know your father and I aren't getting any younger."

"Your mother's right," Dad commented. "I spoke with Dan Laraby the other day and he was complaining about his bones acting up whenever he plays catch with his grandson. You don't want that to happen to us, do you? Your mother and I want to be fun grandparents who can take the kids to games and fairs—not old people who smell like arthritis cream and yell at them to keep the noise down."

"I've only been seeing Adam for a month. We're nowhere even near talking about children."

"But he wants children, right?" Her mom asked. "I mean, who doesn't want children?"

"Lots of people. Robbie, for example," she said, trying not to grin. She did like payback.

"Olivia," her brother warned, but it was too late. Her parents pounced on him.

"What does she mean you don't want children?" Mom burst out.

Though her parents were acting silly, they brought up a good point that she'd been ignoring. She eventually did want to settle down and have a family and Adam was about as opposite to that as she could get. There was nothing wrong with having fun now, but she had to remember not to get too attached. They were just too different for things to work out in the long run.

"And Shoes Emporium and Rebecca's will be delaying their opening as well," Javier said during his daily call Friday morning and Adam sighed. That would bring the total number of stores that wouldn't be ready for the grand opening to six. It wasn't enough to push back their opening date for the first phase, but it would hurt.

"What happened?"

Javier sighed. "The storm. It hit Shoes Emporium's warehouse and delayed a shipment of garments for Rebecca's." And understandably, the two stores wouldn't want to open with a limited offering. They wanted to open with a bang. It was a good thing the movie theater wasn't delayed as well or there'd be serious problems. Adam was banking on the summer's highly anticipated movies to bring the crowds to the new complex. "They should be ready by July," Javier continued.

"I'll be there tomorrow," Adam decided. He'd already been planning to visit next week, but it'd be wiser to go earlier and see for himself just how everything was progressing. He didn't need any more surprises.

Regret filled him when he realized he'd have to cancel his plans with Olivia to watch a show. He wasn't much of a Broadway fan, but he liked spending time with her.

She'd been so excited when she'd invited him. He hated to disappoint her, but business was more important than a show they could watch anytime. Besides, she'd seemed more interested in the architectural designs of the theater than the actual show itself.

"We have a meeting with Stevens tomorrow morning," Javier said, referring to the construction company building the complex. "Do you want me to push it back?"

"No, but thanks for the offer." This was a store problem, not a construction problem, but he'd make sure to attend a meeting with them when he returned for the grand opening next month.

They spoke for a few more minutes about how the second phase was coming along before Adam hung up. He then called his assistant to make the preparations for the flight tomorrow.

Once he was done, he leaned back into his chair and called Olivia. Hopefully, she'd be willing to take a rain check on the show.

"Hey, Adam," Olivia's cheery voice greeted him, making him feel even worse about cancelling their date.

"Hey, Olivia. I'm sorry, I won't be able to make it tomorrow. Some issues have come up with the Plex, and I want to make sure that everything else moves forward without a hitch before we open next month."

"That's all right. I understand."

She was always so damn understanding and, instead of being appreciative, he hated it. How many times had he been late to a date because a meeting had gone on longer than he'd expected?

He'd had these problems with women before, but he'd only cared enough to apologize and to perhaps bring a small token. But it was different with Olivia. He found himself wanting to do better.

It was a crazy notion. He'd never put so much into a relationship—planning dates, thinking of what she'd enjoy, trying to impress her... Frankly, he should've tired of the whole thing weeks ago. Instead, he found himself looking forward to every date.

He thought about his upcoming business trip and how he could remedy the situation. He didn't want to delay the trip, but neither did he want to miss out on spending time with Olivia.

"Come with me?" he asked as soon as the idea popped into his head.

It could be like an extended date. And it had the added benefit of allowing him to show her the Plex. While he enjoyed sharing his work with her, another part of him wanted to impress her. It'd been the same way with the model he'd shown her at the office. He didn't know why, but he wanted her to see him as a successful businessman.

Doubt filled him when she didn't respond, so he added, "We should be back by nine or ten. That is, if you're not busy." She usually spent Sunday mornings with her family, so he knew she'd want to get back before then.

There was a small pause before Olivia answered, "Sure. I'd love to come."

He grinned. He didn't understand how such a simple thing as her accompanying him to Texas could make him so happy, but it did. "Great. I'll pick you up."

They then made plans to watch the show next Saturday and Adam couldn't help but think the day was looking better already.

## CHAPTER FIFTEEN

"So, do you use the same designs for all your complexes?" Olivia asked as they walked around the second phase of the Plex, and Adam resisted the urge to smile. Not only did Olivia seem to be genuinely interested in the project, she looked cute wearing a hard hat, too.

He'd wanted to steal a few kisses from her but knew handholding was as far as she was comfortable with in regards to PDA. And while he loved seeing her blush, he didn't want to embarrass her. Perhaps he'd steal a kiss later when they went back at the trailers where the construction offices were.

"We haven't used the same specs for everything the way others have." There were companies who used the same exact format for everything they built to save time and money. They bought similar plot sizes and built the same building over and over again. "But we often use similar designs and colors for branding reasons." He nodded at the structure. "But the Plex is completely from scratch. Since it's more upscale than my previous projects, I didn't think about branding."

Olivia smiled. "I know of one guy who paints the roofs of all his properties a bright shade of yellow so that he can easily see what he owns when he flies over them."

Adam laughed. "I'm pretty sure I've seen them." He nodded at her. "How about Montgomery? I know the designs can vary greatly from hotel to hotel, but is there a defining feature that all Montgomery hotels have?"

"I can't think of anything design or structural-wise. I guess it's different since we're often renovating older hotels as opposed to building them, but we try to give each hotel its own personality and often draw inspiration from local history. We don't even use the Montgomery brand on all our hotels, sometimes preferring to use the hotel's original name if it has some historical value attached to it or if it's big enough to stand on its own like the Biltmore."

Montgomery's strategy was so different from Stone House's. Stone House had strict guidelines on how every-thing should look and was a stickler for uniformity, often making the hotels indistinguishable from each other. You wouldn't get fancy amenities at a Stone House hotel, but you knew you'd get a comfortable bed and a clean room.

"But if I had to pick a defining feature, I would probably say that it's our customer service," Olivia continued. "We're conscious of the fact that a lot of our customers save for weeks to spend a night at our hotel, so we always do our best to exceed their expectations."

Her reasoning surprised him, but it made sense. When

someone trusted you with their hard-earned money, you did everything in your power to exceed their expectations.

Olivia wrinkled her nose. "I just wished people would stop posting such detailed reviews online. We love to surprise our guests with little baubles or gift baskets—especially if they're celebrating a special occasion. But it's almost come to the point where it's no longer a surprise."

"It's the thought that counts." It wasn't their fault guests were spoiling the surprise for others.

"I know, but still!"

He laughed and realized that he liked having someone so passionate about the hospitality industry and customer service working on The Mansion. But right now, he was more grateful about the fact that her passion had led her to him.

He nudged her shoulder. "Do you want to go to Stanton's for lunch? It's this fusion restaurant my guys have been raving about."

Now that he'd finished his inspection on the first phase and saw no pressing issues, he could relax and enjoy his time with her. He wasn't particularly interested in fusion cuisine but wanted to do something nice to make up for missing the show and as a sign of appreciation for her coming along with him. He would've liked to take her somewhere fun like the space center, but they didn't have the time if they wanted to get back to Manhattan tonight. He'd asked around and from what he'd heard, Stanton's was the place to go.

"Not unless you want to. I'm still full from all those beignets I ate."

Adam laughed. One of his tenants, a coffee shop, was training their employees to make the delicious donuts today and had made enough to feed the whole crew. He guessed he and Olivia had overindulged.

"Let's eat later then," he said, then continued the tour. "When everything is done, we'll have a train ride for children and their parents that'll go around the complex."

"Oh, I've seen those. When I was younger, the children's rides at malls were always carousels." She laughed. "I even had a favorite elephant that I always chose."

He was surprised that her parents had allowed her to ride carousels, let alone go to the mall. His own mom had always harped on about not mixing with the 'common folk.' Instead of going to stores, she'd have the items sent to them. He wondered how she'd react if he told her that one of the families she tried so hard to emulate didn't mind going to malls.

Olivia shook her head as she said, "I still don't know if the rides were meant to draw families in or to appease the children for having to tag along with their parents while they went shopping."

He was about to invite her back when the complex was done so that she could see everything finalized and functioning when he stopped himself. The completion of the second phase was seven months away. It was doubtful they'd still be together by then. He'd simply never dated anyone that long in his life. In fact, Olivia was his longest relationship thus far.

He never got attached to the women he dated and yet, the thought of him and Olivia not being together when the rest of the Plex opened rang hollow. He fought off the wayward thought and answered, "A little bit of both, I guess."

It was no use thinking of things that could never be. He'd never been the long-term relationship type. He just wasn't built for it. But he couldn't help thinking that if he were the type, Olivia would be it for him. Her personality and drive just jived so much with his.

"And this is where our secondary courtyard will be," he said as he nodded at the space between two anchor department stores.

She beamed. "I can already imagine the Christmas tree between the two stores," she said, then turned around. "This is where the Christmas tree will be at, right?"

His chest tightened at the thought of who would keep her warm during those cold winter nights before he pushed the thought away. *Not going there.* "Yes, and we'll have yoga classes in the morning and live music at night."

"Will you run the classes, or will someone rent the space from you?"

"A local dance studio will rent the space for a small fee."

"And you get potential customers when the classes end. Smart."

Pride filled him at her approval. He'd never really sought out the opinions of the women he'd dated before, but he found himself constantly wondering what Olivia thought. The realization that this relationship was starting to become much more involved than he'd expected gave him pause, but he knew it was true. If she wasn't with him, he was constantly thinking about her and when she was with him, he wanted to share everything with her, including the thoughts and ideas he usually kept to himself.

The crazy way he felt about her probably had something to do with their working relationship. He'd always loved his work and it was only natural to fall for a woman who expressed interest in it, but his feelings were going a little too far. He needed to draw the line and keep business separate from pleasure. From now on, he'd keep their business talks focused on The Mansion and would avoid mentioning his other projects.

"Not all the stores will be open by the time the classes end, but I admit we took that into consideration." People could grab a smoothie or a sandwich on their way out. "Come on, let's go check security."

* * *

They were lying in bed one Saturday morning when Olivia turned to face Adam. "How would you feel about meeting my family over brunch?" She didn't really want to invite him, but Mom was getting persistent and she didn't want her parents to feel as if he were avoiding them.

"Sure."

"You don't mind?" she asked, surprised at his easy acceptance.

"I'll admit I've never done the meet-the-parents thing. Hell. None of my siblings have ever brought anyone home except for that one time my sister wanted to get rid of her boyfriend."

"Did it work?"

Adam laughed. "It did. The poor man broke up with Martha the following week. Doug and I were in on it from the beginning, so we knew to give him a hard time. But our parents scared him off all on their own without even knowing it."

"Your parents are that bad?"

"Well, they usually watch themselves when they're around others, but they must've thought Martha's boyfriend beneath them."

"That's awful!"

"Yeah, but it worked out well for Martha. Hey, how about a little quid pro quo? I'll go to your parents' brunch and you'll go with me to my goddaughter's birthday party next month."

Olivia blinked. "You're a godfather?"

He grinned. "Yeah. To a beautiful baby girl. Why do you look so surprised?"

"I don't know. I guess it just seems so domesticated of you." Adam didn't really seem like the family type. Could she have been wrong in her assessment? Unbidden, hope sprang inside her.

"I usually do say no to these kinds of things, but I'm close to the parents."

"To both of them? Did you set them up by any chance?" she asked, intrigued. Maybe he did believe in marriage.

"I wish I could take credit for them, but no. I had nothing to do with their getting together. I went to school with a guy named Jason Collins and kept in touch with him over the years. He eventually opened an investment fund with an acquaintance of his, Luke Darren. And—"

"Wait— You're the godfather of Luke and Samantha's baby?" Olivia asked, surprised.

"Yeah. You know them?"

"Not personally, but I remember their marriage being pretty big news." Luke had married Jason's widow not even a year after Jason's death. Olivia remembered thinking it was sad that someone could move on so quickly.

Perhaps it was naïve of her, but she liked the idea of a love that lasted a lifetime. Stacy, on the other hand, had had the complete opposite reaction and had thought the whole affair romantic. She'd bought into the rumors that Luke had always loved Samantha and had supported her through her trying time.

Adam winced. "Yeah. The press wasn't particularly kind to them. But you'll see once you meet them. They're nothing like the papers were making them out to be."

Olivia remembered. If they weren't making Samantha out to be the lowliest of gold-diggers, they were portraying Luke as some kind of business shark who was only marrying Samantha to gain full control of the company.

"So, do we have a deal?" Adam asked.

"Yes. I'd love to go," she answered, pleased that he wanted her to meet his friends. That had to mean something, right?

"So, how about you? Do you want children?" Adam asked as she settled into his arms again.

"I do, but not anytime soon," she admitted. "I want to be more settled career-wise before starting a family." Maybe once she'd opened a hotel or two, she'd think about it. "How about you?"

"That would be a firm no." He hesitated before adding, "I have nothing against children, but I'm not the biggest believer in marriage."

"Oh," she said, disappointment filling her. She'd already guessed it, but the confirmation was still difficult to hear.

She inwardly groaned as she thought about her parents and how much they wanted grandchildren. She didn't want to give them false hope by bringing Adam over, but it wasn't as if she could withdraw the invitation from him—especially with how fervently Mom had been pushing to meet him.

Not knowing what to do, she just prayed her parents wouldn't take a liking to him.

# CHAPTER SIXTEEN

"Thanks again for coming," Olivia said as they walked through the country club's lobby. It was the third time she'd thanked him, and Adam was starting to get suspicious. Perhaps her family wasn't as perfect as she made them out to be.

"It's nothing. Besides, it's probably the best way to stay on your dad's good side." It wouldn't do if things turned sour before they'd even started the renovation. He knew he should regret risking a business deal—especially one as big as The Mansion—over a woman, but he was enjoying his time with Olivia too much to care.

"I know, but my dad will rely on my mom to ask the things he can't."

"To interrogate me, you mean?"

She nodded. "She's tougher than she looks."

He didn't know why, but he found Olivia fussing over him endearing. "I'll sign the letter H on your palm if I need any help." He doubted he'd need it, but it didn't hurt to be prepared—especially with Olivia worrying the way she was.

"That'll work, but we should probably think of a backup in case my mom separates us."

As they talked about possible signals, Adam glanced around the club his parents had tried so hard to join and was surprised by how warm and inviting it seemed.

He'd been expecting something more along the lines of the club they'd become members of instead, which was full of chandeliers, marble, and stiff-necked waiters. But this was the complete opposite. Along with children's laughter filling the air, the club's wood paneling and the fire it had crackling in the lobby fireplace lent to a warm, homey feeling. While children weren't even allowed at his parents' club unless there was a special occasion.

Perhaps it was because the members of his parents' club were mostly new money that they felt the need to prove themselves. They filled their club with expensive art, creating an uninviting environment for families with young children. But then again, maybe it was intentional. Both kinds of clubs fostered business and political partnerships, but perhaps older clubs such as these focused on a sense of family and community first and business second. The old money could choose who they worked with while the new money often didn't have that luxury.

"Our table is in the back of the restaurant—on the patio," Olivia said as they passed a rotunda and exited the main building. "Since almost everyone in the family prefers a buffet-style brunch as opposed to ordering individually, my dad arranged for the restaurant to set us up our own little buffet."

They reached the covered patio and he saw the family seated at a rectangular table. There were roughly around ten or so of them. From reading every article he could find on Olivia's family last night, he recognized Olivia's immediate family as well as her uncle, aunt, and cousins. He hadn't thought much of it when she'd mentioned that they'd all be here, but now he realized how strange it was that they met so often.

Barbara Montgomery, Olivia's mom, glanced up and beamed when she saw them. "Olivia!" she said as she stood and came to hug her daughter.

Olivia smiled as she returned the hug. "Hi, Mom."

Barbara released Olivia and turned to him. "And you must be Adam," she said as she gave him a warm hug. "It's so good to finally meet you. I'm Barbara Montgomery, Livie's mom."

"Hi, Barbara. It's good to meet you as well. Thank you for inviting me."

"Thank you for coming. I know you're a busy man." She grabbed his arm with a surprisingly forceful grip and led him towards the buffet table. "Let's get some food then I'll introduce you to everyone."

The next hour went by in a blur, with the family talking about everything under the sun and the occasional friend dropping by the table. It was as if he were in one of those Thanksgiving dinners he saw in the movies, but without the fighting. At least not yet. There'd been disagreements, but Olivia and her mom had diffused them before they'd gotten big. Apparently, talking about politics at meals was fine as long as you had a good referee.

All in all, it was surprising to see how well everyone got along. Considering the way his dad had stolen his brother's share of Dannier, Adam had expected to see at least some friction between Olivia's family members.

The Montgomery family owned two businesses, with Victor and his brother each running one. While the hotel business was big, it wasn't anywhere near the size of the bank's, so it wasn't as if they could split the two evenly. Adam didn't know how the ownership of the companies was structured, but judging from the easiness between the two brothers, they were obviously happy with the arrangement. Hell. Even Olivia and her brother seemed to get along just fine with their cousins and Adam got the sense that they really were a tight-knit group.

"So, I have a general manager in mind," Victor said as he dug into his dessert. "Pierre—"

He was interrupted by his wife slapping him on the shoulder. "No business talk during family time," she said and smiled at Adam. "I'm sorry. Victor just lives for those hotels."

Expecting Victor to be irritated by his wife's interruption, Adam glanced at him and was surprised to see the man give his wife a brief smile before he shot him an apologetic look and shrugged.

The couple had been just as warm to each other the whole morning, and Adam had to wonder how much of it was real. His parents did a convincing job of playing the loving couple in front of others as well, but it was a completely different story at home, where they were either giving the other the cold shoulder or screaming at the top of their lungs.

"Now, how long have you and Olivia been seeing each other?" Barbara asked. "Can you believe that I found out from Tamara Blake, who apparently saw you two on one of your dates?" She threw her daughter a hurt look, and Adam couldn't help but smile.

Olivia's mom was something. Her effusive warmth and friendliness hid her strength of character, but it was there just as her determination was. He'd noticed the way she'd maneuvered him into sitting next to her and the way she'd let him settle in before the real questioning started.

"A few months. We decided to keep it quiet, because of our working relationship."

"Months and Olivia never said a thing! I even thought Tammy was mistaken, because all Victor has been talking about was The Mansion this and The Mansion that. I was sure it was a business dinner, but Tammy assured me it was a date."

"Barbara," Victor warned, and Barbara smiled at him.

"I'm blabbing again, aren't I?" Victor nodded, and Barbara laughed as she turned to Adam. "I'm sorry about that. Now, tell me about you."

* * *

Olivia was driving to the office the next morning when Stacy called. "Hey, Stacy! What's up?" she asked at the same time Stacy spoke.

"So… How did it go?"

Knowing that Stacy was asking about brunch yesterday, Olivia sighed. "I guess it depends on how you look at it." Stacy was aware of the concerns she'd had about her parents meeting Adam.

It wasn't that she'd been hoping her parents would hate Adam. Rather, she'd hoped they'd be indifferent towards him. Instead, Mom had liked Adam so much she'd told Olivia she could bring him to brunch anytime.

"I guess that means your parents liked Adam," Stacy said.

"They did."

"Well. That's not really a surprise, is it? I mean, your dad even liked William eventually," she said, referring to Olivia's high school boyfriend. "Not that there's anything wrong with William, but your dad was always calling him a mooch."

Olivia smiled. "Yeah. It didn't matter that we were in high school. Dad expected everyone to work. Now that William has a job, he meets all the qualifications for a son-in-law."

Stacy laughed. "It's the grandchildren bug. Once they see their friends getting grandchildren, they start expecting some of their own."

"It's so frustrating. It's not like mentioning it all the time will make us settle down any faster. They didn't ask Adam if he wanted children, but I could see in Mom's eyes that she'd really wanted to." Olivia felt as if she'd spent half the time staring Mom down, making sure she didn't ask or say anything embarrassing.

"It's crazy. I feel as if I'm a single mom who's worrying about her children getting attached to a boyfriend." It was the first time she'd dated someone who didn't believe in marriage and she found herself out of her depth.

But it wasn't like she could break up with Adam. She could tell herself that it would mess things up with The Mansion again. They'd just gotten a handle on their meetings and them breaking up would certainly undo all the progress they'd made. But the truth was she was falling for him.

"Your parents are adults. They know that not every relationship lasts."

Olivia had known Stacy would say something to that effect, and she had to wonder if that was the reason she'd confided in Stacy the other night, because she'd wanted outside confirmation that it was okay to be with Adam.

"You're right. I'm probably worrying for nothing," she said as she waved at the parking attendant and drove into the underground garage.

"You love your family."

Olivia suddenly realized that she hadn't seen Stacy since she'd joined the family for brunch last month and inwardly cursed herself for being such a bad friend. She didn't want to be one of those women who ignored her friends the minute she got a boyfriend, but it was easy to get lost in Adam. "Are you free for dinner Wednesday?"

"Let's make it Thursday. I have a meeting Wednesday."

"Sounds good."

"Great. I found this great hole-in-the-wall Lebanese place that has the best chicken."

Olivia laughed as she parked in her assigned stall. "You don't even like chicken."

"I know! But I smelled something good and asked the waiter what it was. He said it was the chicken and I just had to order it."

"I can't wait to try it." If Stacy said a restaurant was good, it was amazing. Her friend had great taste.

"I'll text you the details."

After they said their goodbyes, Olivia grabbed her briefcase and headed towards the elevators. She had just passed security and was waiting for the elevator when her phone rang.

She frowned when she saw Kevin Mayer's name on the screen. Kevin was a franchisee who owned the Crown Jewel, Montgomery's hotel in New Orleans. He usually scheduled an appointment when he wanted to talk with her.

"Good morning, Kevin," Olivia said as she answered the phone and braced herself for bad news. Unless they'd won an award, franchise owners rarely contacted her out of the blue with good news.

"I'm sorry, Olivia, I really am, but I just sold the hotel to Tierpoint Properties. I needed the money to prop up my restaurants."

Her stomach dropped as the elevator doors opened and she stepped aside to find a quiet corner to finish the conversation in. She'd known Kevin had been struggling financially for a while now.

He'd been very open about how he'd had to stop the

planned expansion of his fried chicken chain and how he'd even closed a few restaurants due to the fierce competition. Because of that, she'd done her best to help minimize the extent of the renovations to stretch his budget as much as possible, but it hadn't made a difference. Saving a few hundred thousand wasn't exactly helpful when you needed millions.

"That's all right," she said, doing her best to keep the hurt out of her voice. It didn't matter that the hotel was profitable when the owner needed money. At the end of the day, they had to do what was best for them.

Montgomery didn't have the right of first offer for the Crown Jewel, but it still hurt that he hadn't contacted them before making his decision. Then again, Tierpoint had probably approached him. They'd been aggressively adding hotels to their portfolio and were often willing to pay significantly more than the market value.

"I know it hasn't been the best of times," she murmured. Since Tierpoint was one of the biggest Silver Stream franchisees, it was doubtful they'd continue with Montgomery, but she'd still call the new owners tomorrow to see what could be done.

"Thanks for being so understanding. I really appreciate all the work you and Montgomery have done over the years. I'll send in the formal letter regarding the sale with all the details later today. I hope we'll get a chance to work together again in the future."

Olivia shook her head wordlessly as she hung up. She couldn't believe it. She'd spent so much time working on the hotel—from the renovations to the hiring of the managers—and at the end of the day, their competitor would benefit from all her efforts.

She knew what had happened was out of her control. The hotel had been a hobby for Kevin the way others bought horses or yachts, while the restaurants were his passion and had been what he'd made his fortune on. So of course, he'd put the restaurants first. But the reality still smarted and she couldn't help but think that this wouldn't have happened if she had her own line of hotels.

Since Montgomery would own the hotels, she wouldn't have to deal with the whims of franchise owners or the downturns in their other businesses. With franchisees, you could do everything right and still end up on the losing end, and she realized that she couldn't lose focus on her Yosemite hotel. She'd finally found a project her dad could connect with. She couldn't let it fail.

# CHAPTER SEVENTEEN

Adam swallowed as Olivia licked the bit of cream cheese that had gotten on her finger. It was too easy to imagine those lips and mouth on him. She took a bite out of her bagel and he forced himself to focus on his breakfast.

"So, I was thinking we could head to the beach," he said as he dug into his omelette. It was Saturday morning and as much as he'd love to stay in bed with her all day, he didn't want her to think he was only about sex. "We could kayak, paddle board, or stroll along the shore..." Martha had a house in the Hamptons, where she kept just about every single type of water sporting equipment known to man. His sister was the epitome of the work hard, play hard mindset.

"I'm sorry. I meant to tell you last night, but I'll be working today. With everything that's been going on with The Mansion, I've fallen behind on my regular duties."

Damn. He'd really been looking forward to spending the day with her, but he understood. From The Mansion's current operator trying to get everything they could out of the deal to current tenants causing problems, it seemed as if there was always something going on. They'd even had to bump their meetings to twice a week just to cover everything that was happening.

Her Mansion obligations was a whole other job and he wondered why Victor hadn't reassigned more of her duties. Did Victor think she would fail or was this some kind of test to prove herself before he gave her more responsibilities? Probably the latter, Adam surmised, because she was definitely qualified. She could be a perfectionist at times, but that was a good thing in her line of work.

"You could work here," Adam found himself saying. It didn't matter where they were, he wanted to be with her.

"You know we barely get anything done when we work at each other's place. You're just too distracting."

"I'm distracting? You're the one who walks around in only a shirt when I'm catching up on my emails." Not that he minded. He loved seeing her wearing his shirts.

"Hey, you're the one who takes off my clothes minutes after you see me. And I'm not the one who walks around bare-chested."

He grinned. He did love teasing her and especially enjoyed it when she couldn't keep her hands off him. But she had work and, if he were being honest, so did he. Though his team had a good handle on things, he was usually scouting locations for his next complex by now.

But ever since he'd started seeing Olivia, he hadn't been looking as hard. He could tell himself that it was because his money was tied up with the Plex and The Mansion that he didn't want to take any further risks by borrowing even more money. But the simple truth was that he'd rather spend his free time with Olivia than to research new possible developments.

The admission should've scared him. Instead, he wondered why he was always pushing himself so hard. Frankly, he deserved this reprieve with Olivia, and he decided that he'd enjoy his time with her and worry about expanding his business later.

"How about this? You can work in my office today with the doors locked while I work in the living room. I promise not to bother you until you come out." It would be hard to stay away from her, but he'd do it.

She narrowed her eyes. "You'll be working, too?"

Considering that he used to spend most of his free time working before he'd met her, he found her suspicion ironic. She probably thought him a playboy, and while he certainly may have been considered such in the past, he'd matured over the years.

"Yeah," he murmured. "I have a proposal to look at and some other things as well."

"All right," she said, and a sense of relief filled him. *She was staying.*

Adam was reviewing the PR plans for the Plex's grand opening when Olivia walked into the living room.

"It's almost time for dinner," she said. "Did you want me to order something?"

"Sure. What were you thinking of?"

"How about some Mediterranean?" she asked as she sat on his lap and wrapped her arms around him.

"Sounds good to me." He gave her a brief kiss. "Were you able to get everything you wanted done?" Apart from when they'd had breakfast and lunch together, she'd been locked in his office all day.

"Just about, but then again, I always overestimate how much I can get done. How about you?"

"I made a sizable dent in my inbox." As much as he'd missed her company, he was glad he'd been able to catch up on a few things.

A property manager of his had emailed him about one of his tenants not being able to make the rent. The little tidbit had been buried beneath other ongoings and if it wasn't for Olivia deciding to stay in today, he wasn't sure he would've seen it in time. Since Nick's Dry Cleaning was one of his oldest tenants, he'd immediately called his manager. He'd give them a temporary rent reduction but would have to reassess the situation if their problems continued.

Dad would've called him a fool.

He was already giving his old tenants a steep discount in rent and now he'd be temporarily slashing the rent even further for one of them. But it was a luxury he could afford. Since he fully owned AC Developments, he didn't have to worry about reporting to investors or increasing the bottom line.

Olivia glanced down and he realized he was still wearing his computer glasses. Embarrassed, he took them off.

"Why have I never seen you wear glasses before?"

Because he'd avoided wearing them in front of her. He'd never thought twice about wearing the glasses before, but now he was conscious of how he looked to her. It was stupid, but he couldn't help himself.

"It's just for when I have to use the computer," he explained. He often got so lost in research that his eyes would become strained from looking at the screen too much.

"It's a good thing you never bring them to meetings. I'd never get anything done."

"Oh?"

She nodded. "You're already distracting as it is. Seeing you with glasses just turns my mind into putty."

She had to be joking. These glasses weren't sexy. But then again, he didn't think arms were sexy and look how many times he'd caught her watching his. He grabbed his glasses and put them back on.

"So you're saying you find me irresistible with these?"

"Mm-hmmm," she said as she traced small circles on the back of his neck. "They're not bad for you if you're not using the computer, are they?"

Her soft touches short-circuited his brain and he had to think before answering her. "No. They're just to block out glare, so we're good."

Her lips curved into a sensual smile. "Good," she murmured before bending to kiss him. The taste of her filled him as their tongues mated. She softly bit his lip and he groaned. Keeping her legs wrapped around him, he stood. *Bed.* He needed a bed for all the things he wanted to do to her.

Her hands greedily roamed his back as she deepened the kiss. He couldn't get to his room fast enough. He turned on the lights as he walked in and settled her onto the bed. He quickly made quick work of her shirt and was greeted with the sight of her magnificent breasts. Groaning, he took one into his mouth as he filled his hand with the other, licking and tweaking the nipples to his delight.

She moaned his name as her nails dug into his back. He released her nipple, then peppered kisses down her stomach as his hands explored her body. He undid the buttons on her pants, then removed them along with her black panties.

Arousal hit him hard and fast as he opened her legs and saw her glistening folds. She was always ready for him. He lowered his mouth and felt her tremble beneath him as he ate her. Grinning, he took his time, licking and nibbling, loving the way her moans filled the air.

She screamed his name as she came. Tightening his hold on her legs, he kept on, not letting up until she came again. He eased his ministrations as she settled down, then stopped to glance up.

Smoky eyes looked back at him and he grinned. "Aren't you glad you decided to stay?"

"I'm still deciding," she teased.

"Then I better get moving." He stood, and she laughed.

He dispensed with his clothes, enjoying the way she watched him with those dark eyes of hers. He loved that she seemed as fascinated with his body as he was with hers. He returned to bed, crawling back into her open arms, and kissed her. He entered her, her hot sheath engulfing him, and he groaned. Damn. He could never get enough of her.

Pleasure built to incredible heights as they moved against each other. Her legs encircled him and he nearly came. Gritting his teeth, he continued his strokes. But the sensation soon became too much when he felt her coming, her tight walls squeezing him, her moans turning him inside out… He followed, thrusting into her until he was completely spent.

A deep satisfaction filled him as he plopped down next to her and gathered her into his arms. Life was good. The only thing that could make it better was if she never left. He was about to ask her to move in with him when he caught himself.

What the hell was he doing?

Sure, the sex was amazing, and he loved spending time with her, but wanting her to move in with him? That was the first step to settling down and he was definitely not going there.

He wished he could tell himself that the coziness of today had gotten to him, but he knew he'd be lying to himself. The more time he spent with her, the more he craved. It had started out with him just wanting to spend the nights with her. Now, a few months later, he wanted to spend all day with her as well. He could still remember how disappointed he'd been when she'd said she wanted to work at home this morning, then how relieved he'd been when she'd changed her mind. Somewhere along the way, his sense of happiness had begun to depend on her, and it scared the shit out of him.

Was this how his parents' relationship started?

He'd never been able to understand the way they allowed the other to hurt them, but if the highs were this good, then maybe they thought the lows worth it. Not wanting anyone to ever have that kind of power over him, he knew that he'd have to back off before Olivia came to mean even more to him.

Because there was no way in hell he'd end up like his parents.

---

# CHAPTER EIGHTEEN

---

"Strength Fitness approached us about allowing our guests access to their gym," Olivia said to those gathered around the meeting room table as she moved on to the next item on her checklist two weeks later.

She'd been planning to hold off discussing this particular topic until the end of the meeting, but Ricky had brought up the idea of adding a restaurant to the top floor of the hotel, which would reduce the amount of meeting space area they had planned. She wasn't particularly fond of the idea of using an outside gym, but it would allow for the additional restaurant without compromising meeting space. Besides, it was her obligation to let their partners know about opportunities like these. "I've included their plans for the gym in the folder."

"They'll be opening a location down the block from us," she continued as everyone turned to the appropriate papers. "There wouldn't be direct access to the hotel, but it would allow us to have more revenue-generating space and the guests would have access to a swimming pool at the gym."

"Does Montgomery have any deals with gym providers in your other hotels?" Adam asked as he glanced up.

For what seemed to be the umpteenth time that day, she tried to see if there was something different in the way he acted towards her. She hadn't seen much of him these past two weeks due to his "busy schedule," and she couldn't help but wonder if he was making excuses to avoid her.

Seeing nothing unusual, she answered, "Only in San Francisco, but Razor Gym was built inside of the hotel, so it's convenient for our guests."

Perhaps he wasn't interested in her anymore. It would certainly explain his being busy all the time. Her chest ached at the thought. While she'd been falling deeper into him, it seemed he'd been tiring of her.

"And you think having to go out of the hotel is inconvenient for the guests," Adam said, and she nodded.

"I do. They'd either have to go out in their workout clothes or bring another set of clothes. But I do think Strength's pool is something to look into." She knew pool access was a deal breaker for some, but there simply wasn't room for one in The Mansion. Hopefully, they could come to an agreement with Strength to allow their guests to use the gym's pool.

"Okay. See what you can do."

She nodded, then turned to Ricky. "And I'll talk with Seth to see what we can do about the restaurant." They then began going over Prism's list of maintenance requests and her recommendations for them.

Once the meeting was over, Olivia turned to talk to Adam, but he was already talking with Ricky. Not knowing how long their conversation would take and whether or not they wanted privacy, she headed towards her office.

She was probably worrying for nothing. Sure, she hadn't seen much of Adam lately, but he'd been just as attentive as ever the few times they'd gotten together. She sighed. She used to spend all her time working and now it seemed as if all she could do was think of him. Perhaps she should take a page out of his playbook and start focusing on work as well.

She had just turned on her computer monitor when she heard Adam's voice. "So, I'll see you later?"

Her heart skipped a beat as she looked up and saw him standing at her doorway. The warmth from his smile spread through her, easing her concerns. *He really had just been busy.*

"That's what I was planning."

"Lasagna and chicken good?"

She laughed. "It better be. Cynthia's probably already preparing it," she said, referring to his cook. "Besides, everything she cooks is divine."

"I'll let her know you said that," he said with a twinkle in his eye and just like that, she wanted to kiss him. She often regretted their agreement to hide their relationship in the office, especially at times like these. *Why did he have to look so damn good in a suit?*

"Well. I better get going," he said as he released his hold on the doorway. "Ricky's waiting for me."

"I'll see you tonight."

"Don't bother changing. I have plans for that dress." His

statement caught her off guard, but before she could respond, he grinned and left.

* * *

Satisfaction filled Adam as he read Javier's report on the Plex. The theater and a few of the stores had opened ahead of the grand opening and, despite a few hiccups, things were going so well that one of their parking structures was almost at full capacity. It was too early to call the project a success, but it was definitely off to a good start.

His team had really stepped up to the challenge—especially with all the delays and issues that had come up, and he couldn't be prouder. Many of his employees had been with him since the earlier years and seeing them grow was an amazing thing.

He thought of his first assistant, Sylvia Lee, who'd been as tough as nails on the phone and as shy as a mouse in person when she'd first started working for him. Over the years, she'd gained more and more confidence and was now in charge of his PR team. Javier had started out as an intern and now, headed new developments. And there were so many more.

Adam often gave his employees yearly Christmas bonuses, but he wanted to do something more to reward those who had been with him for a long time. He vaguely remembered his accountant talking about profit-sharing a while back and decided to look into it after the grand opening.

Remembering the last time he'd gone to Houston, he

smiled. He must've traveled to Texas hundreds of times, but Olivia's presence on the trip had made it one he'd never forget. From stealing kisses to showing off his work, he'd had a blast and he suddenly realized how much he wanted her at the grand opening. Furthermore, he'd be in Houston for the next two weeks and he simply didn't want to go that long without seeing her.

He knew she wouldn't be able to get away for the whole week, but he wouldn't mind flying back and forth an extra time if it meant she could come. He hadn't seen much of her these past few weeks, though admittedly, that was his own fault. He'd been afraid of how much he was coming to rely on her and had pulled back.

But at the end of the day, it had been his loss. All the time he'd spent missing her was time he could've spent with her. With the decision to invite her made, he picked up his phone.

"Hey, Adam," Olivia's cheery voice greeted him.

"Hey, Olivia. How do you feel about going with me to Houston again in two weeks when we have our grand opening?"

There was a pause before she spoke. "I'm sorry. I have a lot of work to catch up on."

Disappointment bit at him, but he understood. Work didn't stop just because you were seeing someone. And while he admired her dedication, he couldn't help but be jealous of her work. He'd been looking forward to showing her the complex when it was filled with people.

He shook his head. Exactly when had he become a show-off? Olivia was certainly doing strange things to him.

"How about tonight?" he asked. "Do you want to go to Il Tarzano?"

"I'd love to, but I really do have a lot of work. How about tomorrow?"

"Sure. I'll pick you up at six."

Adam frowned as he hung up a few minutes later. Though he'd been the one to take a step back these past few weeks, Olivia had never complained, and he realized how much that bothered him. He guessed a small part of him had been hoping that she'd demand more of him, demand that he put a bigger priority on their relationship. Instead, she'd always been understanding, saying that she had work as well.

And though he knew that was true, his instincts told him that there was something more, something that he was missing. Was it possible she didn't care one way or another if she saw him?

His heart stopped at the thought. It would explain why she never complained about his hours or his absence. They used to spend most nights together and now he only saw her once or twice a week. Yet, she'd never said a word.

It hurt to think that she didn't feel the connection he did. Of course, he knew that their relationship would end eventually, but he just wasn't ready yet. It felt as if they'd only gotten started and sometimes, he had the odd feeling that he'd never tire of her. Damn. He hoped he was wrong and that she really was just busy. Because he didn't know what he'd do if she called it quits.

# CHAPTER NINETEEN

Olivia frowned as she looked at her calculations. She'd gathered the old financials of a few hotels that Montgomery had taken over to see if the business had improved once they'd reopened as a Montgomery and if so, by how much.

She'd been hoping she could use the numbers to estimate how The Mansion would fare after the renovation. It was easy to see that business—by way of revenues and occupancy rate—had improved across the board for all the hotels, but other than that, the numbers were all over the place. The occupancy rate had increased anywhere from two to thirteen percent and the revenue disparity was even larger.

How in the world was she supposed to decide what figure to use for The Mansion estimates? Wondering if she'd miscalculated the numbers somehow, she started redoing her calculations.

She was meeting with one of Montgomery's accountants tomorrow to go over the numbers she didn't understand

and she wanted to use the time wisely. She still had a few months before Seth finalized his designs and her dad expected a finalized budget along with the projections, but since finance had never been her strong suit, she needed to start preparing now.

Because now that she was in charge, she'd be the one answering the questions. Her head throbbed at the thought. She was already having a hard time estimating the occupancy rate. She didn't even want to imagine how she'd handle the cash flow calculations.

Her doorbell rang. Thinking that it was Adam, she smiled before she remembered that she'd told him she'd be working tonight. Frowning, she checked her phone and saw William Yates at the door.

"Just a sec," she told her ex through the app that was connected to her doorbell's camera. Wondering what William wanted, she stood and headed towards the door. She opened it and caught him shifting from foot to foot, as if he were unsure of his welcome.

Wanting to put him at ease, she smiled. "Hey, William," she said as she hugged him. "Long time no see." They'd been friends before they'd started dating and, though they hadn't had the friendliest of break-ups, she hoped time had alleviated any bad feelings between them.

"Hey, Olivia," he said and shook his head as he took a step back to look at her. "Wow. You look amazing."

"Thanks. You look good, too."

There was an awkward pause before he nodded at her. "Can we talk inside?"

Her curiosity spiked. Aside from that awkward time

when he'd pushed hard for them to get back together and the few times they'd run into each other, they'd never really shared anything more than the "Merry Christmas" or "Happy Birthday" text since they'd broken up more than five years ago.

"Sure. Do you want something to drink?"

"No, thank you," he said as he walked in. "I don't know how else to say this, so I'm just going to blurt it out. I'm engaged."

His announcement caught her off guard. Considering how much of a party animal he'd been in college, she guessed she'd always expected that she'd settle down before he did. Instead, she was seeing someone who didn't even believe in marriage. Shaking off the wayward thought, she hugged William again.

"Congratulations! Who's the lucky girl?"

"Penelope Hunter."

"Any relation to Charlie Hunter?" she asked, referring to their old schoolmate.

"His sister. It'll be hitting the press soon, but I thought you should know."

She wasn't hurt by the news, but she appreciated his thoughtfulness to spare her feelings. "Thanks for telling me."

He sat on her couch, frowning. "You know, I always thought we'd end up marrying."

Years ago, she had thought so too—as probably did most teenagers with their first love. At the time, everything felt as if it would last forever.

"We were so young when we started seeing each other,"

she said as she sat next to him. "It probably would've been jaded to think that we wouldn't last." But they hadn't even been able to make it through their second year of college.

She could still remember how relieved she'd been when he'd broken up with her. By then, he'd felt like a burden— another responsibility she'd had to handle on top of her never-ending schoolwork. He'd wanted to go clubbing practically every night while she couldn't even keep up with her homework. They hadn't been able to understand each other, which had led to constant fighting. He was such a contrast to Adam, who'd even let her use his office to work.

"I still regret how things ended between us," William said.

"It all turned out for the best. You're getting married and I have an amazing boyfriend."

"You're seeing someone?"

She nodded, smiling. "Yes. I'm—"

"Olivia!" Adam's voice boomed outside before three bangs sounded on her door. "Open this door right now!"

* * *

A red haze filled Adam's vision as he pounded on Olivia's door. Thoughts of Olivia with the man who'd entered her house filled his head and he boomed, "Open this door right now!" He and Olivia were finished, but he'd be damned if she slept with the man right under his nose!

It was no wonder she'd never complained about him working. She'd already found a replacement. He'd called himself crazy when he'd parked down the street from her brownstone earlier—a fool for not trusting her. But he'd known something wasn't right and had decided to stake out her house anyway. He hadn't even been here thirty minutes when this man had shown up.

He was about to pound on the door again when it opened. "Adam, is everything all right?" Olivia asked, as if nothing was wrong.

"Is everything all right? You blow me off to be with him?" he asked as he gestured towards the man behind her. And to think, he'd actually believed her when she'd said she had work.

She frowned. "William showed up unexpectedly."

Yeah, and that was why she'd been so happy to see the guy. The image of her embracing the other man still burned in his mind, churning his gut.

"Er. Hello," the man in question said as he offered his hand and Adam ignored it as he stepped inside. He wasn't about to shake the hand of the man she was seeing behind his back. "I'm William Yates. I was just dropping by to tell Olivia some personal news."

"He's getting married," Olivia said. William gave her a look and she shrugged. "What? You said it would be announced soon and it's not like Adam's going to spread the news." After a moment, she sighed. "Fine," she said as she turned towards Adam. "Don't tell anyone. It hasn't hit the papers yet."

Adam was too angry to respond. He couldn't believe Olivia was making up stories instead of admitting the truth. Did she think she could continue seeing the both of them?

"Would it be all right if I invited your parents?" William asked, continuing the act, and Olivia smiled.

"I'm sure Mom would be pleased."

As if asking if it was safe to leave her there with Adam, William subtly tilted his head in Adam's direction as he looked at her questioningly, enraging Adam further. He'd never been a violent man, but he seriously wanted to beat William to a pulp right now.

Olivia nodded. "Thanks for telling me. I really appreciate it."

"All right. I'll see you." Frowning, he glanced at Adam, then left.

Olivia locked the door and turned towards Adam. "You thought I was cheating on you, didn't you?"

"Are you going to deny it?"

Her lips pursed. She looked as if she were about to say something before she shook her head and opened the door. "I think it's best if you left, too."

"So you can let William back in? What kind of a fool do you take me for?" He'd stay here the whole night if he had to. It wasn't rational to try to keep them apart, but he just couldn't stomach the thought of Olivia with someone else right now. He and Olivia had had something special—or so he'd thought—and those feelings didn't suddenly disappear because she was seeing someone behind his back.

"A really big one if you think I'm cheating on you." She closed the door and shook her head. "I've never cheated on anyone in my whole life. Why would you even think that? I've never given you reason to suspect me of cheating. I still can't— Wait, have you been cheated on before?"

"I've never—" He stopped when he realized he was about to say that he'd never been in a relationship long enough to be cheated on. He'd look like a fool if he told her the truth—that before her, he'd never had a relationship last longer than a weekend. "I've never been cheated on," he said firmly instead.

"And yet you think I'm cheating on you." She gestured towards him. "I guess that means you're cheating on me because it's usually the accuser who's the cheater. That's why you've been so 'busy' lately," she said, using her fingers to make air quotes.

"I really have been busy," he said, though he knew he could've made the time for her.

He'd been afraid of how she made him feel and had pulled away. And it had been the right call, even if his justification for doing so had been off the mark. He inwardly shook his head. How long had she been cheating on him? How had he not known?

"And don't turn this on me," he continued. "You're the one who said you were busy when you were really seeing someone else."

"I told you—William dropped by out of the blue to tell me he was getting married."

"And why couldn't he do that through a call or a text? Why did he have to do it in person?"

"Because he was being considerate and didn't want me to find out through someone else. We used to date."

Adam's jaw tightened as he remembered the way William's eyes had consumed her. The man was obviously still interested. "For how long?"

She folded her arms. "Almost four years—from high school to college."

"And you wanted to what? Get back together?" Because why else did the man have to tell her he was getting married? Adam inwardly cursed himself. Why was he even considering her lies?

Olivia had him so wrapped around her finger that he wanted to believe her. Afraid of losing her, he was desperate to latch onto any explanation for what he'd seen just so that he could continue seeing her. More fool he.

Her eyes narrowed. "No. But you know how it is with your first love. There's always going to be a connection—a certain fondness—even if it's not love anymore."

He ignored the idea of her having a connection with William. The idea was anathema to him. "You said you were working tonight."

"I was before everyone decided to drop by!" She gestured towards the dining table, where stacks of reports were piled around an open laptop. "Why did you anyway?" A beat passed. "Wait a minute. You were watching my house?" Her voice rose incredulously. "You were watching me? I can't believe this! What could I have possibly done to make you think I was cheating on you?"

He was about to deny it before he realized he didn't have to. Considering that he'd found a man in her house, he had nothing to feel guilty of. He'd been right to be suspicious.

"You've been avoiding me."

"And because of that, you—" She shook her head. "I can't do this. Just go."

His jaw tightened. She wanted him to leave? Fine. So be it. He wouldn't stay here and listen to her lies, praying that she was telling the truth. Without saying another word, he turned and left. They were done.

* * *

Olivia shut the door and screamed in frustration. Ugh! She couldn't believe the nerve of that man! Because she'd chosen to spend more of her free time working, he thought she was cheating on him?

She'd only been following his lead. He'd been busy working the past few weeks and she'd taken the opportunity to catch up on her own work. Because no matter how differently she'd acted these past few months, her life didn't revolve around him. Just because he was suddenly free didn't mean she'd drop everything for him. She'd understand if he was disappointed, but to spy on her and then automatically assume she was cheating on him?

How could someone she cared so much about think so lowly of her?

They were well and truly over. Even if he did apologize, what kind of a relationship could they have if he couldn't even trust her? Her chest ached at the thought.

Deep down, she'd known their relationship had been doomed from the start—he didn't believe in marriage and children while she wanted it all. But she'd ignored the warning bells, because she'd wanted to be with him so much and now, reality was rearing its ugly head. She had no one to blame but herself.

She blinked back tears but couldn't stop them from falling. Given the awful way Adam had acted, she should be glad to be rid of him. But she wasn't. She wanted him to come back and tell her that it had all just been one big misunderstanding—that he'd never believed she could cheat on him. Knowing that wouldn't happen, she sobbed harder.

When her tears finally subsided, she went to wash her face. As she dried herself with a towel, she thought about the ramifications of their breakup. Considering the way Adam had looked at her, she doubted he'd let her stay on the project and, unfortunately, he had final say since he had majority rule.

For pride's sake, it would be better to quit than to be fired, but she'd be damned if she quit on her grandfather's hotel. No. If Adam wanted her gone, he'd have to fire her himself.

She just prayed he'd keep his accusations to himself. Dad would undoubtedly back her up if Adam accused her of cheating, which might cause Adam to pull out of the deal completely. And she did not want to be the reason for her dad losing another Manhattan hotel, especially when it was The Mansion.

She groaned. She should've never gotten involved with Adam.

# CHAPTER TWENTY

Anger fueled Adam as he ran on the treadmill early the next morning. Sure, he'd known his relationship with Olivia wouldn't last forever. But he'd never thought she would cheat on him. She was always talking about how important family and loyalty were and, all the while, she'd been going behind his back!

She wasn't who he thought she was, and the smartest thing for him to do would be to forget her.

It was easier said than done.

It didn't seem to matter that she was a cheater. All he could think about right now was how much he missed her. He tried to tell himself that she was just one woman in a line of many but knew he was lying to himself.

If she were like the other women, he wouldn't be having such a hard time concentrating on work or going to sleep. Instead, her betrayal had kept him up all night with a crazy mix of emotions that had left him both wanting to curse her and make love to her. Disgusted with himself, he'd headed to his gym in the hopes of burning off his anger.

But it wasn't working. He'd just finished his fourth mile and he was still fuming.

He couldn't believe she'd tried to pull the wool over his eyes. Even his parents didn't do that. No. They flaunted their indiscretions to the other, striking where it hurt the most. But Olivia hadn't even admitted it.

He frowned at the thought.

Judging from last night, he figured Olivia had never wanted him to find out about William. So if she hadn't wanted to hurt him with her cheating, why had she cheated at all?

Could it have had something to do with The Mansion?

Or worse, had she only been with him because of the hotel? His stomach churned at the thought. He'd never felt this way about anyone before and if it turned out she'd only been with him, because of business… No. He wasn't even going to go there.

*But what if she was telling the truth?*

He shook off the wayward thought that had been flitting through his mind since leaving her place. Just because he wanted to believe her lies didn't make them true. If anything, his wishful thinking just showed how deeply she'd gotten under his skin. He wanted to continue their charade of a relationship, because the thought of never holding her in his arms again brought on a sense of emptiness that was too much to bear.

It was ridiculous. He should be grateful that he'd figured out the kind of a person she was before he got even more involved, but all he could think about right now was how much he missed her.

*I've never cheated on anyone in my whole life.*

Her words from last night rang in his head and oddly enough, he realized he believed her. He slowed the treadmill as he allowed himself to think about what he'd seen.

She'd opened the door and embraced William without a single hesitation. He'd been too far down the street to see if they'd kissed, but her lipstick hadn't been smudged when she'd opened the door and their clothes hadn't looked disheveled or wrinkled…

*Was it possible they'd just been talking?*

Perhaps, but judging from the way William had looked at Olivia, he wanted to rekindle their relationship. Thankfully, Olivia hadn't looked at him in any particular way. Adam still hadn't liked the easiness between the two, but he wasn't about to let an ex scare him off.

His chest lightened at the realization that he was going after her. Considering the way he'd acted, Olivia might not take him back, but he had to try. Besides, from what she'd said, he'd know sooner or later if William was really engaged or not.

* * *

Unease coursed through Olivia as she walked towards her brownstone and saw Adam sitting on the steps. Though he hadn't called or texted, a part of her had known he'd come today. But now that he was actually here, she didn't know what to expect. Was he going to apologize for the way he'd acted or was he going to say he couldn't work with her?

As if sensing her, Adam looked up and stood. "Olivia."

She reminded herself to be cordial. Adam wasn't just an ex—he was an important business partner, too. "Hi, Adam. Have you been waiting long?"

"A little. I wasn't sure if you'd see me."

"It's hard not to when you're sitting on my stoop," she said, purposely misunderstanding him, as she walked up the stairs. Sighing, she opened her door. "Come in."

Once they were inside, he started, "I'm sorry. For every-thing." She should be relieved that he was owning up to his mistakes, but all she felt was anger. She hadn't deserved the way he'd treated her. She'd done nothing wrong. "You've been busy lately and then seeing you with William…" He shrugged as he shook his head. "It just reminded me so much of my parents and their affairs that I snapped."

Though he'd told her about some of the bad things his parents had done, this was the first time he'd spoken about their marriage. Suddenly, his behavior during the brunch with her parents made sense. He'd been fun and charming like always, but he'd also kept looking at her parents, as if he were expecting something to happen.

Given that his parents cheated on each other, it wasn't hard to imagine their home filled with strife, and she now realized that Adam had probably been searching for signs of tension between her parents. Perhaps, he'd even been expecting a fight or an argument of some kind.

"I'm sorry to hear about your parents," she began gingerly. "I can't even imagine how hard that must've been for you growing up. But just because they cheat doesn't mean everyone else does as well."

"I know, and I'm sorry."

"Well, I appreciate you coming here to apologize." Unfortunately, it was too little too late.

He hesitated before he spoke. "So, this is it, then?"

Her throat tightened as she nodded. "I can't be with someone who doesn't trust me. You didn't just barge into my house, thinking that I was cheating on you. You spied on me." She'd always thought it would be romantic for a man to get jealous over her, but the reality was downright depressing. It wasn't love that motivated the jealousy. Instead, it was insecurity and possessiveness.

"I know it may not look like I trust you, but I do. I just don't seem to see reason when it comes to you. I—" He shook his head. "Friends?"

She blinked. "You want to be friends?"

"I want more than that, but I'll take you any way I can have you."

"I don't think I can. I'm just going to end up falling for you again." Especially when he said things like that.

"Why don't we take things slowly? We can go to my goddaughter's birthday party this Saturday and see how things go from there." When she didn't respond, he added, "You did say you would go."

She should refuse. She had absolutely no defenses when it came to him and would only get hurt again. But they *had* made a deal. It was bad form to go back on her word, especially when she wanted him to see her as trustworthy.

But she knew she was just making excuses. She wanted to go. It was as plain and simple as that.

"Okay. I'll go to your goddaughter's birthday party with you, but I make no promises—friends or otherwise—after that." Hopefully, she wasn't making too big a mistake.

He smiled that smile she loved so much, and she knew she was in trouble. "Great. I'll pick you up at ten."

* * *

Guilt dug into Adam as he made his way towards William Yates's office the next day. Olivia wouldn't be pleased if she found out that he'd paid a visit to her ex, but he couldn't leave things up to chance.

She may have forgiven Adam for his actions the other night, but she hadn't taken him back. And while Adam tried to change her mind, the last thing he needed was for her ex to jump in, trying to edge him out.

Adam had seen the way William looked at Olivia and knew that, no matter what Olivia said, things were far from over on William's end. Why else would he have dropped by to say he was getting married? A man only did that when he was still interested in a woman. Olivia was just too innocent to see it.

Knowing he couldn't risk any loose ends, Adam had called Edward as soon as he'd gotten home last night, asking the investigator to see what he could find on William. Edward had called back less than thirty minutes later. Apparently, William was the son of some cable mogul, making the search a lot easier.

Adam ignored the curious stares as he made his way across the office and found the door with William's name outside. Without knocking, he barged in and saw William on the phone. The man's eyes widened as he murmured, "I'll call you back," to whomever he was talking to, and hung up.

"Stay away from Olivia," Adam said at the same time William spoke.

"How the hell did you get in here?" William asked, then laughed when he heard Adam. "You do know that I'm engaged, right? To Penelope Hunter. You know, Hunter as in the Hunter Broadcasting Company."

"Engaged or not, I don't want you anywhere near Olivia." Based on the sappy eyes William had made at Olivia, he'd drop his engagement in a heartbeat with just the slightest encouragement from her.

William's chin lifted. "Or you'll what?"

"Or I'll tell your fiancée that you visited Olivia."

"Penelope knows that I'm inviting Olivia to the wedding," William answered smugly.

"Yes, but does she also know about you wanting to get back with Olivia?"

William's face flushed with anger. "She told you?"

Adam's lips twitched. Olivia hadn't, but he'd had a hunch. Judging from William's reaction, she'd obviously turned him down, which meant that she hadn't cheated on him. His chest eased at the thought. He'd been hoping, but he hadn't been completely sure.

"What about the wedding?" William asked. "Olivia's expecting an invitation."

Adam lifted a shoulder. "Things get lost in the mail."

"And her brother's and parents' invitations, too?"

"Lousy wedding planner." It wasn't his problem. He nodded at the man. "This better be the last time I see you." He turned and left, pleased with the confirmation that Olivia hadn't been seeing William behind his back. That alone had made the visit worthwhile.

Seeing William's eyes bulge in fear? Well, that had just been the icing on the cake.

# CHAPTER TWENTY-ONE

"Adam! Thanks so much for coming!" Samantha Darren said as she approached, holding her daughter, Suzie, in her arms. Though he didn't believe in the institution of marriage, it was plain to see that it suited Sam. She'd been so thin and sad after Jason died. Now, she was practically bursting with happiness.

"Of course. I wouldn't miss Suzie's birthday for the world," Adam said as he tickled the baby's stomach. Suzie giggled, and he smiled. "And this is Olivia Montgomery," he said and took the opportunity to wrap his arm around Olivia.

There'd been a palpable strain between him and Olivia on the drive over. It was as if she'd suddenly put up these walls around her and he hated it. He missed the easiness between them and hoped his casual touches would help warm her towards him.

"Hi, it's so good to meet you," Sam said as she shook Olivia's hand.

"It's nice to meet you as well. You have a beautiful home."

Copying her mom, Suzie lifted a hand towards Olivia. Olivia smiled as she shook it. "And it's nice to meet you, too!"

As if Olivia passed some kind of test, Suzie laughed and lifted both arms at her. Sam nodded at her. "Do you mind?"

"No. Not at all."

Sam handed Suzie over. "Aww, she's precious," Olivia said as the baby smiled in her arms and Adam couldn't help but notice how soft Olivia's eyes had gone. He'd known she wanted children, but the reminder still stung.

He might be willing to change his mind about marriage, but parenthood was a firm no. He never wanted to put a child through what his parents had put him and his siblings through. And while he liked to think he could be a better parent than either of his parents were, he couldn't be sure. Hell. Look at how he'd acted when he'd thought Olivia had been cheating on him. He'd never thought he was the jealous type, but apparently, he was. Big time. Frankly, he didn't think clearly when it came to her and he could easily see himself doing anything he could to make her stay with him—including using any possible children they may have.

"We think so, too," Sam said, breaking into his thoughts, and he was grateful for the distraction. He'd never understood how his parents could act the way they did, but after having first-hand experience of how crazy Olivia made him, he was beginning to gain some insight. "Come on. Let's sit in the shade before she gets too heavy."

Adam eyed all the decorations and chafing dishes as

they approached the tent. "It looks like you have a big party planned."

Sam laughed. "There's probably only going to be twenty people. But with it being Suzie's first birthday and all, Luke went a little overboard. He even hired someone dressed up as the R-A-B-B-I-T from her favorite cartoon as a surprise."

They were about to sit down when Sam said, "Excuse me. My parents are here. Please help yourself to the buffet. Luke should be down any moment. He's just showing off the new crib his dad made." Olivia passed Suzie back to Sam, who then made her way towards the older couple.

"She's a lot nicer than I expected," Olivia said once Sam was out of earshot, and Adam laughed.

"I told you the press had made the situation sound worse than it really was."

"Yeah. I should've known better, but it was such a juicy story. Now, I feel bad for gossiping about them. Luke is probably just as nice as Sam." She nodded at him. "Did you want to go find him, by the way?"

He normally would've, but there was no way he was about to leave Olivia's side. He'd been looking forward to spending time with her for days. "He'll come down eventually. Come on, let's see what they're serving."

* * *

"Hey, Olivia, did you get cake?" Samantha asked as she plopped down next to Olivia almost two hours later.

Olivia nodded. "I had two slices already." She'd only

meant to eat one, but it had been so good she hadn't been able to resist when the waiter had offered her another slice.

Samantha smiled. "This is my second one, too," she said before taking a bite.

"So, Adam mentioned that you started your own investment fund?" Olivia asked after a moment.

Samantha nodded. "Mostly for my parents' friends and some family members. Not understanding the risks involved, a lot of them wanted to invest with Luke." Samantha gestured towards her. "You probably know what that's like."

While Montgomery Bank did manage various funds, Olivia had never had people ask her about how to invest with them. Probably because most of the people in her circle were already acquainted with either her brother or her uncle, both of whom were far more knowledgeable about these things. But she could definitely understand where Samantha was coming from—especially if her parents' friends didn't have anyone else they could turn to in the finance world.

"I tried pushing them towards an index fund," Samantha continued. "But they're more comfortable with someone they know managing their money for them. How about you? Luke mentioned that you work at Montgomery Hotels?"

"Yes. I'm the relations manager for our franchisees. I'm actually working with Adam on The Mansion right now."

"Oh, I love the tearoom! My friend—Nina—you met her, right?" At Olivia's nod, Sam continued, "She just took me to tea there last year and we literally felt like royalty."

Olivia beamed. "That was actually my grandfather's goal for the hotel. He wanted guests to feel like royalty and drew inspiration from European castles." He'd mixed and matched what he liked about the different structures and had called the results the best of the best.

"I don't mean to be nosy, but did you sell Adam the hotel then agree to manage it?"

"Oh, no. My grandfather sold The Mansion in the eighties to save the family's bank during the crisis." He'd originally wanted to take a loan against the hotel, but with the tight credit market, it just hadn't been possible.

"I was curious because I've been reading up on Key Hotels and I've seen them sell a hotel, only to continue managing them."

"I'm not too familiar with Key Hotels except for their experimental programs." Key's investments to bring technology and artificial intelligence to the forefront of the hospitality field often made headlines. "But it's a common practice in the industry." In fact, most publicly traded hospitality companies focused on their franchise business as opposed to actually owning hotels. "In addition to companies culling the lower-performing locations or shifting their main business focus, there's just more money to be made in franchising than actually owning a hotel." She shrugged. "But in Key's case, I think they're experimenting with different hotel features to see what works." It wasn't enough to offer a clean room and a comfortable bed. Hotel brands, especially the low- to mid-tier ones, needed to constantly reinvent themselves to set themselves apart from the competition. "They probably had the hotel designed with a certain program in mind and when it didn't go the way they were hoping, sold the hotel. That way, it doesn't look like a failure and they get continuous income from the franchisee." She smiled. "For existing properties, it's practically free money." Little risk was involved, and the hotel was already designed to their standards.

"Which is why some brands are almost all franchises."

Olivia nodded. "Did you hear about those robot assistants they tested?" she asked, referring to Key's failed trial to use robots to deliver small items to rooms. She knew Montgomery would never do anything like that, but it was still fascinating to read about.

"Yes! I was excited when I read about it. I know it was a bust, but I hope they bring it back in some form or another in the future. There's just so much potential in the technology."

They then talked about the various ways hotels were reducing costs—from limiting housekeeping and toiletries to double booking rooms. It was often hard to think about what the other hotel brands were doing. It was just so different from how Montgomery operated. While everyone was moving from mini shampoo bottles to wall-mounted dispensers, Montgomery still included toothpaste in their toiletry sets.

It was times like these that made her grateful her family had kept the company private. Because of that, they weren't constantly worried about making bigger profits to satisfy shareholders and could just focus on improving the customers' experience.

A baby cried in the distance and Samantha murmured, "I better check on that."

"Feel free to call me if you ever have any questions about the industry," Olivia said as she handed Samantha a business card. "I love talking shop."

"I'll do that," Samantha said as she stood. "It was nice meeting you. You and Adam have to come for dinner one of these days. It'll be nice not to be the only woman for a change."

Before Olivia could say she and Adam were just friends, Samantha left and went to help the mother with the crying baby.

Olivia frowned as she watched Samantha lead the woman and baby inside the house. What did Samantha mean by saying she was usually the only woman at dinner? Was she saying that Adam didn't usually bring his girl-friends over or that Adam didn't usually date? The thought that she might mean something to him had hope leaping through her. Maybe that was why he'd been so jealous of William…

And there she was making excuses for him again.

She sighed. Adam had just been so attentive today that it was easy to see why she'd fallen for him. Though to be fair, he'd always been an attentive boyfriend. Perhaps too much, she thought as she remembered the fact that he'd spied on her. It hadn't been the first time a boyfriend had been unhappy about how much she worked, but it had certainly been the first time she'd been spied upon and accused of cheating.

Frowning, she tried to put herself in his position. How

would she have felt if she'd seen a beautiful woman leave his apartment? She liked to think that she wouldn't have automatically assumed he was cheating, but she wouldn't have been happy—especially if she'd found out the woman was an ex-girlfriend of his.

But then again, she would've never spied on him to begin with.

Though it was probably easier for her to trust than it was for him, given the way he'd described his parents. And apart from that night, he had been the perfect boyfriend…

She sighed at the realization that she was going to give him another chance. She'd probably regret it, but a part of her worried she'd regret it more if she didn't.

* * *

"Thanks for helping," Luke said as Adam placed the last gift inside Suzie's playroom.

"Anytime," Adam said as he straightened. He'd offered to help when he'd seen his friend carrying a big box, only later realizing that Luke had probably wanted to get away from all the people for a while. Luke wasn't exactly the sociable type.

"So, how've things been going?" Luke asked as they walked back to the party.

"Good. We're going to have the grand opening for the Plex in a couple weeks and everything's going as planned with The Mansion. How about you?"

Luke grinned. "We haven't told anyone yet, but Samantha's pregnant."

Adam gave Luke a big pat on the back. "Aww, man. Congratulations."

"Thanks. I still can't believe how lucky I am." Luke shook his head. "You'll understand when you have a kid."

Adam didn't bother telling him that he wasn't the white picket fence kind of guy. Ever since Luke had married Sam, he seemed to think it a given that Adam would settle down as well. And while Adam had sometimes found himself envious of their love, he knew that that kind of a relationship just wasn't in the books for him.

He was saved from answering when Olivia approached them. He smiled as he put his arm around her. "Are you ready to head back?"

She nodded, and Luke spoke. "All right. I won't keep you. But I hope to see you for dinner soon. Both of you."

"Sure. Thanks." Though Adam didn't want to go out with them, he was happy Olivia had hit it off so well with his friends. He'd never really cared about what his friends thought about the women he saw, but he'd found himself desperately wanting Luke and Sam to like Olivia. And they did. With Luke being the introvert he was, he wouldn't have invited her to dinner if he didn't want to.

But Adam wasn't entirely comfortable having dinner with Luke and Sam. If he was being honest, he hadn't been comfortable around them since they'd started seeing each other. Sometimes the looks they gave each other were just unnatural. He could almost swear love was pouring out of them.

It was funny. He'd never had this problem when Samantha had been married to Jason. But seeing Sam and

Luke so happy together made him think about things he shouldn't, like what would happen if he were the type to settle down?

And now that he'd met Olivia, the feelings had only worsened, because he could imagine settling down with her if he were a different man. Whether in bed or out, he loved spending time with her and doubted he'd ever tire of being with her.

But at the same time, she made him feel and it wasn't all good. It was as if his emotions were a hundred times more intense. He couldn't remember ever being as happy as he was with her, but she also made him crazy, like when he'd found William at her house. He should cut his losses and let her go. Instead, he found himself inviting her to the Plex's grand opening again.

"I'll be flying to Houston on Monday and will be staying there until the grand opening," he said as they walked through the house to the driveway. "I know you're busy, but I would love for you to be there when it opens."

"It's two Wednesdays from now?"

"Yeah. Let me know your schedule if you're available, so that I can have the jet ready." He'd been hoping she could come a day or two earlier, but it was better for her to be there one day than not at all.

"You don't have to do that."

"I know, but I want to."

"All right. I'll see what I can do." She laid a hand on his chest and kissed him. The kiss was all too brief and left him wanting more. Wrapping an arm around her, he kissed her properly, sweeping his tongue against hers, relearning the taste of her. It had only been a few days since they'd last kissed, but he never wanted to go that long without kissing her again. She licked her lips as they pulled away. "Let's go back to your place."

It took a moment for her words to register and when it did, his chest eased. She was giving him another chance. *Thank goodness.*

# CHAPTER TWENTY-TWO

Olivia frowned as she looked at the proposed floor plans for the residences as she and Adam flew back to New York Wednesday evening. It looked a little small for what were supposed to be luxury apartments. Even the smallest residences should be at least twenty-five hundred square feet.

Curious as to how that would fit, she got a ruler and scale from her bag then began experimenting with different room configurations. She was just seeing how a two-story residence would fit next to a one-story residence when Adam spoke.

"We'll be touching down soon."

Surprised, Olivia glanced up to see it was fully dark out. "Thanks for letting me know." Time flew when she designed—especially when she played around with iterations.

"What are you working on?"

She lifted the diagrams. "I'm just trying to see if it would make sense to make the residences bigger."

"May I?" he asked.

She nodded and handed them to him. He took his time as he flipped through the sheets. "These are really good."

Her cheeks warmed. "Thanks. Laying out the rooms by hand helps me think."

"You know, it's never too late to go back to school."

"I know, but I just don't see it mixing with my duties at Montgomery." It was only a matter of time before Dad approved one of her Yosemite proposals and that would be the start of a whole new line of hotels.

The adventurer branded line wouldn't grow to the size of Montgomery's flagship brand, but it would strengthen the core business by introducing their brand to a whole slew of new customers. And the chance to grow the company that had come to mean so much to her was just too big of an opportunity to throw away by resuming her studies.

"Well. At least you were able to use what you learned," Adam said as he returned the diagrams and she packed up. "Thanks again for coming."

Olivia smiled. That had to be the tenth time he'd thanked her today. "Thank you for inviting me. I had fun." She'd been wondering if their reconciliation had been a mistake. His distrust had really hurt her and she wasn't sure how they'd bounce back from it. But he'd been trying to make up for it ever since and she appreciated the effort.

Though he'd been in Houston, he'd sent her presents almost every day to let her know he'd been thinking about her. Even now, when he should be in Texas, working, he'd taken the time to fly back and forth to accompany her to the opening. He'd said he needed to get a few things done in the office, but she suspected he could've done them remotely.

And he'd been just as attentive during the grand opening. She'd thought she'd have time to check her messages and emails throughout the day, but he hadn't let her out of his sight. If he hadn't been touring her around the shops, he'd been introducing her to everyone he could.

She'd loved seeing him in his element. Not only was he passionate about his work, but he really cared about the people he worked with. It was evident in the way his employees acted towards him. Even when they were busy, they'd always treated him with respect and, many times, even admiration. They wouldn't have acted so if he wasn't a good boss.

But she guessed she'd been subconsciously looking for a crack in his behavior—something that she'd missed that would explain his uncalled-for-behavior a few weeks ago. She hadn't found anything, and since she was usually a good judge of character, she had to believe his reaction was an outlier.

She just prayed that he could learn to trust her because, despite the pain he'd caused, she still cared deeply for him. And considering a future without him? It was too much to bear.

* * *

A sense of contentment filled Adam as Olivia slept on his shoulder on the drive back to her place.

The past two weeks away from her had been hell. On top of missing her, he'd constantly worried she'd change her mind about giving him another chance. But she hadn't voiced any doubts and had seemed to enjoy spending the day with him. Her falling asleep on his shoulder was just the icing on the cake to the perfect day.

He was probably making it a bigger deal than it really was, but he liked to think that it took a certain amount of trust to fall asleep on someone's shoulder and was glad for the tinted partition blocking the driver from seeing them. He'd never been much of a private person, but he was quickly finding that there were some things he wanted to keep between Olivia and him.

Smiling, he went back to checking the news on his phone. It was just past seven and traffic was almost at a standstill. But instead of being irritated, he was glad Olivia was finally getting some rest. They'd left at three in the morning to catch an early flight and had been on the go ever since.

He was just reading about a development company that was planning a net-zero energy shopping complex when Olivia stirred. She smiled adorably as she looked up at him.

"What time is it?" she murmured.

"It's a quarter 'til eight."

"Oh, do you want me to order dinner?" she asked as she straightened.

"Sure." He would've done it himself, but he hadn't wanted to be presumptuous.

"Pizza at La Cucina?" she asked as she got her phone.

"Sounds great."

He went back to reading as she placed the order. He'd just finished the article when he received an incoming call. He was about to put it through to voicemail when he saw that it was his father and hesitated. There'd been a missed call from him earlier as well, which Adam had been planning on returning tomorrow. But what if something was wrong?

"It's my dad," he explained to Olivia before answering the call.

Before he could say anything, his father spoke. "Where have you been? I've been at the lobby of your apartment building for the past hour, trying to get a hold of you."

His dad was at his apartment? "I just got back from Houston," he answered, confused. Dad had never been to his apartment before.

"We need to talk."

Adam inwardly groaned as he glanced at Olivia. He'd been looking forward to spending the evening with her, but he couldn't ignore the urgency in his father's voice. "I'll be there in an hour."

"An hour! I've already been here—"

"I'll see you soon," Adam interrupted. It wasn't like he could control traffic. Shaking his head, he hung up. "I'm sorry, Liv. I'll just be dropping you off tonight. My dad's waiting at my apartment."

"Do you want to go straight to your place? I can call and have the food rerouted there."

He thought about it. While he didn't want her to see how messed up his family was, he wanted her there for support. The realization surprised him. He was becoming reliant on her and he didn't like that one bit. He used to be perfectly fine whenever he'd had to check on one of his properties, and now, he wasn't happy unless she was with him. The thought was terrifying. He didn't want to rely on her for his happiness and the fact that he already did made him pause and reconsider.

"Thanks for the offer, but I think it's best if I met my dad alone." Pain flashed in her eyes, triggering a tightening in his chest. Hating that he'd hurt her, he added, "I'm sorry."

"It's all right." She threaded her fingers with his. "Call me if you want to talk."

# CHAPTER TWENTY-THREE

Adam stepped out of the elevator and found his dad sitting in one of the lobby chairs. The doorman winced when he saw him. "I'm sorry, Mr. Campbell, but he was most persistent in staying."

"That's all right. I understand." Adam knew Justin would've called security if it had been a total stranger who wouldn't leave. But on top of Adam looking a lot like his dad, a quick online search would've confirmed Mitch Campbell as his father.

Adam turned towards his dad, who'd approached while he'd been talking with Justin, and froze. He'd never seen Dad look so frazzled. Dad hadn't shaved and his hair looked as if he'd run his hand through it a hundred times.

Unsure of his father's intentions, Adam had been planning on taking him to a nearby coffee shop to talk, but seeing him so out of it changed his mind. Adam tilted his head towards the elevator. "Come on."

"I need a loan," Dad said as soon as they were in the

elevator and the doors closed. "Dannier's up to our neck in debt. Our loans are maturing and we'll be forced to file bankruptcy if we can't repay them."

Adam blinked. Out of everything he'd thought his dad would say, he hadn't been expecting that. Not wanting to think of what-might-have-beens, Adam had purposely kept himself out of the loop regarding Dannier, but he'd always imagined the company doing well.

"How did this happen?" he asked when he finally found his voice. It wasn't like Dannier was a capital-intensive business. Hell. Knowing Dad, he was positive the company was still using the formulas Grandpa had created. So if they weren't spending money on R&D, what exactly were they spending the money on?

"The competition is getting fierce in the industry. It seems like every week there's a new cream that's all the rage. We've had to cut our prices just to maintain our market share while our costs have been increasing steadily."

It was a strange statement to hear from his dad. Mitch Campbell was all about reducing costs and expenses. In fact, all the disagreements Adam could remember his dad having with either him or Grandpa regarding Dannier had stemmed from the fact that Dad pinched every penny to maximize profit margins.

Dad watched the company's expenses like a hawk. If he wasn't rejecting ideas for new products because of the R&D costs, he was trying to streamline the assembly line to speed up factory production. Time, Dad had constantly drilled into Adam's head, was money. Because of that, Adam simply couldn't imagine a scenario where his dad would've maintained their overhead while simultaneously cutting their prices.

Still having a hard time processing everything, Adam headed towards the coffee table as soon as the elevator doors opened. He grabbed a notepad and a pen, then asked his dad for some numbers.

He shook his head when his dad was done. The company would need at least forty million and that didn't include what it would take to turn the company around. Something like this didn't happen overnight and he suddenly realized that that was why Dad had called all those weeks ago. He'd known he'd need help and had wanted to start buttering Adam up.

As much as Adam wanted to tell his father to get lost, Adam loved his grandfather and owed everything he had to him. And Dannier had been Grandpa's life—his legacy. Dad had often said that Grandpa loved the company more than he had his family and he hadn't been joking.

"I'll think about it," Adam finally said. Investing in Dannier or giving them a loan might just be delaying the inevitable, but he couldn't stand by and do nothing. He'd never forgive himself.

His grandparents had done so much for him. He couldn't betray their kindness by turning away from the company they'd worked so hard to build. In the back of his mind, he realized that this was probably how Olivia felt about The Mansion. It was no wonder she was willing to fight so hard to preserve it. "Did you bring any financials?"

"No," Dad said, and Adam sighed. His dad was asking for help yet he was still hiding information.

"I can't make any decisions without looking at them."

"All right. I'll send them over."

"And all your reports—sales, account receivables, payables, everything."

His dad's jaw tightened before he nodded. "I should've listened to you and expanded our product offerings when we had the chance."

After all the hours he'd spent trying to change his dad's mind, Adam should've felt vindicated by the admission. Instead, he just felt sad that the company that had meant so much to him was in shambles.

"It is what it is," he said and hoped his dad wouldn't try to have a heart-to-heart. The timing was just too suspicious to think him sincere. Thankfully, his dad took the hint that he wasn't in the mood to talk and left shortly after.

Once his dad was gone, Adam sighed. Though he'd been angry with his parents for a long time, he'd never wanted to see them fail. In a way, he'd liked competing with them, even if it had only been in his head.

He briefly wondered if there'd been anything he could've done that might have prevented Dannier from sinking so low before he crossed the thought off. With Dannier being solely owned by his dad, it wasn't as if Adam would have had any real say in the company even if he had chosen to stay involved.

He ran a hand through his hair and resisted the urge to call Olivia. It was crazy how much he wanted to talk with her—how much he needed her. How had he allowed her to get so close?

And the fact that he hadn't even thought about flaunting their relationship to his father stunned him. She was Olivia Montgomery—of the Montgomery family. His dad would've been falling over his feet to meet her. But Adam had come to truly care for her. He couldn't use her that way.

But he had hurt her.

Remembering the flash of pain in her eyes, he grabbed his phone. He'd apologize and tell her what had happened. She deserved at least that for all that she'd done for him today. Still, he'd gotten in too deep with her and needed to take a step back from their relationship and put some distance between them while he got his emotions back under control. Thankfully, this whole mess with Dannier would give him a reason for the space he needed.

* * *

Olivia sighed as she put the food on the counter and headed towards her bedroom. She suddenly wasn't hungry.

Because Adam was always pushing to spend more time with her, she'd foolishly thought that there was something growing between them—something real. But he didn't even care enough about her to introduce her to his dad. It didn't matter that he and his father didn't get along. The man was still his father and Adam cared enough about him to meet him at a moment's notice.

Adam may send her gifts and introduce her to his

friends, but when it came to the stuff that really mattered, he pushed her away and she had to wonder if he'd ever truly let her in. Probably not, she figured given that he'd believed she was cheating on him—a sure sign that he hadn't taken the time or made the effort to truly get to know her and a sure sign that their relationship had only been superficial for him.

And perhaps that was a good thing. It wasn't in her best interest to make a serious commitment right now. If she got her wish, she'd soon be building the first of what she hoped would be many hotels all over the country. She didn't want to be tied down to anyone. She should be relieved that Adam wasn't looking for anything more serious.

But she wasn't. If anything, she felt as if her heart was breaking into two.

Her phone rang, and she saw that it was Adam. "Hi," she said, making the effort to keep her melancholy thoughts out of her voice.

"Hey—I'm sorry I didn't invite you back with me, but my dad is just something else."

"That's all right. I understand." She wouldn't push him if he didn't want to be pushed.

He began telling her about the situation with Dannier and his dad. She was surprised to hear that the company was doing so badly. She'd always thought cosmetics were a steady business.

"What are you going to do?" she asked once he was done. She wished she could give him a big hug, but he didn't want her there. Her chest ached at the thought.

"I honestly don't know. Dannier obviously has a big problem."

"You didn't know they were struggling?"

"No. I've been avoiding anything that has to do with my parents." Considering what he'd said about them, she understood. Every bit of news would just be a reminder of what he'd lost when he walked away.

"I'm sorry. I know how much Dannier means to you."

"Thanks. I need to call my accountant to see what my options are, but I wanted to let you know what was happening."

As they said their goodbyes, Olivia knew she should be happy that he'd cared enough about her to call. Instead, she couldn't help but think this was the beginning of the end.

# CHAPTER TWENTY-FOUR

Adam watched as Jake Halliday, once again, shook his head and flipped to the next page of Dannier's financials. With his limited knowledge of finance, Adam had figured getting an expert's opinion would help him understand the extent of what he was dealing with.

He had no problem valuing real estate and properties, but didn't have a clue when it came to valuing businesses. He would've normally asked Luke for help, but he and Samantha had gone to San Francisco to meet with a few tech companies. Judging by Jake's reactions, Adam wouldn't be surprised if he announced the financials were some of the worst he'd ever seen.

Sighing, Adam thought about the calls he'd made to some of the Dannier employees he remembered from his youth. It seemed as if everyone had different explanations as to why the company had gone downhill. One person had blamed the company's aggressive expansion policy, another had blamed the new cream formula, another had blamed the low pay… But no matter who he'd talked to, everyone agreed that the company had been grossly mismanaged.

After what seemed to be forever, Jake handed him back the financials. "Run."

"That bad, huh?"

"Yeah. If it's the employees you're worried about, I would recommend waiting until the company files bankruptcy then buying all the assets. It would be a lot easier and cheaper to start anew than trying to fix this hot mess."

Adam had thought of that, but he didn't want the company his grandfather had built to get a bad name. His grandfather's memory deserved better than that.

"Roughly speaking, how much would it cost to turn this around?"

"After bankruptcy?"

"Without," he answered, and Jake whistled.

"Assuming you get the right management team and everything goes right, maybe seventy million? And that's being really optimistic." Jake frowned at him. "You can't seriously be considering this, can you?"

Adam shrugged. "It's my grandfather's company."

"And you can buy the name in bankruptcy."

But it wouldn't be the same and he'd know it. He was beginning to understand why Olivia had been so adamant about keeping certain things the way they were at The Mansion and suddenly felt guilty about the way he'd been unwilling to compromise at times. It had just been business to him while, for her, it had been about preserving a legacy.

"I'm still thinking about it. It's a lot of work that I don't really have the time for." He had his own responsibilities and people to take care of. "But there's this guy—Alfred Thompson. He was my grandfather's right-hand man at the company. If anybody can turn the company around, it's him." Though it had been fifteen years since his grandfather had died and Alfred had worked at the company, the basics of the business were still the same. "Of course, I'm not sure if he's willing to come back. My dad fired him almost immediately after he took control."

"I'm guessing this Alfred wouldn't have let your dad bleed the company."

"My dad probably felt threatened by him," Adam admitted. "Alfred would've taken over the company if he hadn't been there, so by firing Alfred, Dad thought he was securing his position."

But his father really had bled the company dry. Adam inwardly shook his head as he thought about the way his dad had complained about having to cut their prices to keep up with the competition. The first thing Adam had noticed when he'd gotten the financials was that Dannier was paying off two jets. And though that didn't account for all the losses they had, the lavishness was an indicator as to how Dad ran the company.

It was still hard to believe that the person who'd rejected Adam's idea for a men's product line because of the R&D costs would spend the company's money so wastefully as to authorize the purchase of a second jet, but the numbers didn't lie.

"Thanks for taking a look at these. I really appreciate it." He'd been hoping for better news, but had known it was a long shot.

"It's nothing. I always enjoy getting a peek into the financials of private companies."

"Any luck finding a buyer for Gerard?" he asked, remembering their conversation from a few months ago about the chocolate maker. But in the back of his mind, he was already thinking about how he was going to come up with the money to save Dannier.

It was a foolhardy thing to even consider, but he couldn't deny that returning to his roots held appeal. Running the company had been his childhood dream and, though he'd avoided all talks of Dannier these past few years, he still cared deeply for it.

Jake sighed. "We decided to take it off the market until the economy improves. The offers we were getting were so ridiculously low that it just made more sense to keep it."

"How's the management?"

"Good, but the president is looking to retire in the next year or two."

They spoke briefly about the pros and cons of hiring a successor from within the company versus bringing in someone from the outside before Adam thanked Jake again for his time.

As he left Jake's office, Adam called his assistant to schedule a meeting with his team. He needed to start working out exactly how much it would take to keep Dannier running and whether or not he could afford another loan.

* * *

Adam frowned as he followed his car's GPS directions to Alfred Thompson's house the next day. It seemed as if each neighborhood he passed was worse than the last. He was beginning to think there was some kind of mistake, but as he'd learned with the rumors Doug had inadvertently started, Edward didn't make mistakes.

The GPS led him to a single-story house. With its white paint peeling away and rotting porch posts, the house had definitely seen better days. Guilt pricked his conscience at the knowledge that his father had done this to Alfred and Adam couldn't help but wonder if there'd been anything he could've done. Sure, he'd only been in high school at the time, but he'd still been Dad's favorite son and the reason why Dad had full control over Dannier. Knowing he couldn't do anything about the past, he pushed the thoughts away and grabbed the folder from the passenger seat.

As he neared Alfred's house, Adam saw that while it might not have a fresh coat of paint, it was still loved. The fence wasn't broken like he'd seen in some of the properties along the street and the yard was well-kept. There was even a small vegetable garden. Perhaps Alfred's wife took care of it. He vaguely remembered seeing her at parties.

Adam rang the doorbell but didn't hear a sound from within. He waited a few seconds, just in case, then knocked on the door.

"I got it!" A male voice boomed followed by footsteps. "I don't know you," the voice said behind the door.

"Hi. I'm looking for Alfred Thompson. My name is Adam Campbell. I'm Richard's grandson."

The door opened, revealing an older Alfred than he'd last seen. Alfred had probably been in his early- to mid-forties then and now, he was well into his fifties.

Adam smiled at the familiar face. "Hi, Alfred. Long time no see."

"Little Adam?" Alfred's face broke out into a grin as he opened the door wider and stepped out to wrap an arm around him. "How are you doing? I heard you're some hot-shot developer now."

"I'm doing okay."

Alfred laughed as he waved him off. "And how about your sister? I haven't seen you all since—" He frowned and Adam guessed he was probably thinking about how Adam's father had fired him.

Not wanting Alfred to think about the bad times, Adam said, "Martha's doing well. I was wondering if I could talk to you about Dannier."

Alfred threw him a look. "That was a lifetime ago."

"May I come in?"

Alfred nodded, and he walked in. "I don't know if you've heard, but Dannier is in really bad shape."

"Like I said, that was a long time ago."

A feminine laugh drew his attention and Adam looked up to see Alfred's wife walk into the room. "A long time ago, my ass. He's always talking about how he would've done this or that. Just last week, he was telling me how Dannier should've made hair products."

Adam smiled. "That actually makes sense. I've heard about people mixing the moisturizer with their conditioner." He offered the woman his hand. "I'm Adam Campbell, Richard's grandson."

"Denise Thompson," she said as she shook it.

Alfred cleared his throat and nodded at the folder in Adam's hand. "Is that for me?"

"It is." Alfred took the folder, then sat down to read it.

"Would you like anything to drink?" Denise asked.

Adam shook his head as he took a seat. "No, thank you."

"Then I'll leave you two to it."

When Denise left the room, Adam started, "They're close to filing bankruptcy, but I'm thinking about stepping in. If I did, would you be willing to help?"

Alfred froze. "You want me to act like an advisor to you?"

"No. I want you to run it."

Alfred laughed as he shut the folder. "I'm an old man. Those days are long behind me."

"You look fine to me and there's no one who knows this company better than you do."

"And how does your father feel about this? You know he fired me, right?"

"I do and I also know that that wasn't what my grandfather intended." If Grandpa had had his way, he would've undoubtedly had Alfred continue his role as vice president for as long as Alfred wanted. Though Grandpa had been proud of Dad's business prowess, he'd always gotten along better with Alfred because they'd shared a similar outlook on business.

They'd both prioritized new products and had been

content to take a more cautious approach regarding the company's global expansion, entering one country at a time, studying each market thoroughly before entering it.

They would've never taken the aggressive approach his father had and entered multiple countries simultaneously. In order to maximize profits, Dad had scaled everything from production to advertising. He'd been successful at first, penetrating the Latin America market easily, but his venture into Europe had failed horribly.

Though there were similar competing products in Europe, Adam couldn't help but wonder if Dannier would've been successful if they'd just taken a more cautious approach. Dad's methodology worked spectacularly when it worked, but it didn't leave any room for failure.

"Besides, it doesn't matter what my dad thinks. When I make my offer, I intend to acquire full voting rights." He wouldn't let his dad have any say in the company he'd run down.

Alfred hesitated before he handed him back the folder. "I appreciate the offer, but I'm not a miracle worker."

Well, at least, he understood how tough a job this was going to be. "I'm not asking you to perform any miracles, Alfred, just your best." Adam smiled. "We can even make those hair products you were thinking about." The fact that Alfred was still thinking about these things only solidified Adam's decision that he was the one to run the company. Dannier needed someone who was passionate about the company and Alfred was it.

Alfred laughed. "I knew I always liked you."

"So, is that a yes?"

"I haven't been in the industry for a long time," Alfred said after a minute.

Adam nodded.

"I know." From the investigative report, Adam knew that Alfred's last job was as a bookkeeper for a car dealership and could read between the lines. His dad had fired Alfred without recommendation, and Alfred had never found another job like his previous one. "But I don't think the industry's changed that much, either. I mean, sure, a lot of our customers were bought out by the bigger retailers, but the products and the underlying business are still the same."

Alfred was thinking about it when Denise's voice filled the air, "If you don't say yes, I'm going to smack you."

Alfred laughed and said, "Then I guess it's a yes."

Adam smiled as he shook Alfred's hand. "You won't regret it."

# CHAPTER TWENTY-FIVE

"I'm sorry, Adam, but we can't offer you a loan for Dannier," Barry Kline said over the phone, and Adam sighed. With Dannier's state of affairs being what they were, he'd known getting a loan would be a long shot, but he'd had to try.

"How do you feel about taking another loan against AC Developments?" the banker asked. "We can do it at the same rate as before."

"I appreciate the offer, but I can't." He'd already been hesitant about the loan he'd taken to get The Mansion deal done, but the opportunity had been too good to pass up. And he certainly didn't want to be reckless the way his dad had been with Dannier. Sure, things were going great for AC Developments now, but there were no guarantees in business—especially with how sensitive housing prices and shopping centers were to the whims of the economy.

"I understand. How are you getting along with The Mansion?"

"Good. We're still finalizing the design, but our preliminary cost assessment is on track with our budget."

"That's fantastic news," Barry said before launching into a discussion about the state of the commercial real estate industry in the tri-state area.

Once they'd disconnected, Adam pulled up a spreadsheet that listed all his investments and their estimated market values. At the top of the list were The Mansion and the Plex. Selling one of them would be enough to cover Dannier's expenses for at least two years, but as it was the last time he'd looked at the spreadsheet, he didn't want to sell either. He'd been there from day one with the Plex and he just knew that The Mansion would be a success once they'd renovated it.

His investments with Luke as well as his smaller properties were below, and he tried a few configurations. He could sell the whole Star complex along with two other shopping complexes... But the Star was the first complex he'd ever built. Many of the tenants had been with him since the beginning and he felt as if he had a certain responsibility towards them. If he sold the complexes, he'd feel as if he were turning his back on them.

A lot of the tenants were mom-and-pop stores and not all of them would survive if the new owner raised their rent to current market levels. He knew he was being soft-hearted, but he couldn't forget how they'd put their trust in him when he'd been a nobody.

He *could* put some kind of rent control clause into the contract terms, but he'd have to justify that with a lower selling price. He ran a hand through his hair as his thoughts veered towards The Mansion. He'd originally wanted it for revenge against his parents. But wouldn't gaining control over Dannier and turning it around be a much sweeter revenge?

And yet, he wasn't happy. Instead, he wondered why revenge had felt so important and wished his dad had come to him sooner about his problems at Dannier. If he had, their losses might've been manageable enough that he wouldn't have had to sell any properties. But Dad was prideful and had wanted to keep up appearances as long as he could.

Adam frowned. Selling The Mansion was truly the way to go. Not only would he be able to continue taking care of his tenants and his employees, but he also knew that the hotel would be in good hands with Montgomery. The fact that he'd, in all likelihood, get a good price and a quick sale made the option all the better.

And he'd make Olivia happy. She'd love for her family to fully own the hotel again. He'd miss working with her, but perhaps it was for the best. He was starting to get too attached to her—always wanting to call and see her. Hell. He couldn't go an hour without thinking about her.

Hopefully, selling his half of the hotel would give him a better sense of distance and would draw the line between their business and personal relationships. He just wasn't sure he wanted to.

* * *

Olivia was heading towards the meeting room when her cell phone rang. She perked up when she saw Adam's name. With him being busy with Dannier, they'd barely had the time to talk this past week.

"Hey, Adam," she said as she stepped to the side to take the call.

"Hey, Olivia. I just wanted to let you know that I'm going to offer my share of The Mansion to your dad later today."

Her stomach dropped at the realization that he wasn't calling for personal reasons until his words sunk in. "Wait, you're offering to sell us your share?" He'd been so adamant about not selling the whole hotel to Montgomery.

"Yeah. I need to free up some cash if I want to invest in Dannier."

"I thought your friend said that it was basically throwing good money after bad." She knew he'd been serious about saving the company, but she was surprised that he was willing to let go of the project that had a much better chance of success to do so.

It was Kevin Mayer and his fried chicken chain all over again. The business might not be the moneymaker it once was, but it was the one he was passionate about.

"It probably is, but I'll never know if I don't try."

And Montgomery would get The Mansion. She should be ecstatic at the news. It had been what she'd wanted for so long. Instead, all she could think about was how the sale would affect their relationship.

"I'm sure your grandfather would be proud of what you're doing and thanks for letting me know. I appreciate it." At least, she wouldn't be blindsided when her dad told her, and she took comfort in the fact that Adam had been considerate enough to give her a heads-up. "Are you going to tell my dad your reason for selling?" She didn't want to say anything she wasn't supposed to if her dad asked her.

"I'm not planning to, but you can tell him if he asks." A few beats passed before he spoke again. "I've missed you."

She smiled. "I've missed you, too."

"I don't know what time I'm getting out of the office tonight. The team is still working on an offer for Dannier, but let's have dinner tomorrow."

Relief filled her at the realization that their relationship wouldn't end just because their business one was about to. They made plans for him to pick her up after work tomorrow before disconnecting and she made her way towards the meeting room.

* * *

It was almost four in the afternoon when her dad called her into his office.

"I just got a call from Adam saying that he wants to sell us his stake in The Mansion," he said as she walked into his room. "Is everything all right between you two?"

"Yes, but he's looking into bailing out Dannier."

Dad laughed. "From what I heard, Adam and his father don't exactly get along."

Olivia smiled. It figured that Dad would've looked into Adam before going into business with him. Character was important to Dad—so much so that he probably knew more about Adam's personal life than he did the actual details of their business deal.

"They don't, but it is his grandfather's company."

A speculative gleam entered her dad's eyes. "I hope my grandchildren would do the same if Montgomery ever runs into any trouble." He was like a dog with a bone when it came to grandchildren and it had only gotten worse after she'd started seeing Adam.

"I rather hope no one ever has to be put in that position again," she said, thinking about how Grandpa had sold The Mansion to save the family bank. It had hurt, but he'd done it for the family.

"I know you think Grandpa selling The Mansion was all bad, but I doubt Montgomery Hotels would be here today if he hadn't. He'd been content to have just the one hotel. But after the way he was able to prop up the bank with the proceeds from the sale, he decided that the family's wealth couldn't depend on just one industry. After things settled down with the bank, he returned with a vengeance and quickly opened three hotels within five years. And the rest is history."

"Grandpa never put it that way."

Obviously, she'd known about him opening the later hotels, but he'd never said anything about why he'd wanted to or how doing so diversified their investments. All the stories he'd told her were more along the lines of how he'd imported the finest marble for the floors of The Mansion or how he'd dash to the hotel during his lunch break to make sure that an important diplomat checked in without a hitch. Then again, she'd only been a child and probably wouldn't have understood it if he'd talked about business strategies.

Her father laughed. "Your grandfather was a ruthless businessman in his prime, but as he got older, he softened and became more sentimental. That building had been in the family for ages—first with the bank and then with the hotel. Even though selling the hotel was the right decision, he'd hated that he'd lost the building under his watch."

"And now it'll be fully back in our hands. That is, if Adam's offer is to your liking," she said, realizing that she shouldn't take the sale as a given. At her father's nod, she breathed a sigh of relief.

"This certainly calls for a celebration," her dad said. "What do you say about dinner at the hotel?"

It was such a change from the days when he'd forbidden her from going to the hotel that she couldn't help but smile. "I'm in. Let me call Robbie."

* * *

Olivia was responding to an email from a franchisee who wanted to open another hotel when she heard two raps on her office door. Thinking that Adam had gotten out of work early, she smiled as she looked up. "Hey—" She stopped when she saw William.

Her ex smiled as he gestured towards the door. "I just had a meeting with my lawyer downstairs and thought I'd drop in and say hi."

"Prenup?" she guessed. She had no doubt William did an amazing job when it came to dealing with his clients, but doubted he dealt with any legal matters. He had absolutely zero patience when it came to the minute details.

"Dad insisted," he said, and she had to stop herself from shaking her head. He was letting his dad make his decisions for him the way he had his whole life, and she had to wonder if he'd ever grow up. He was almost thirty, for goodness' sake! He should be able to make these important decisions on his own.

Though the situations were different, she couldn't help but compare him to Adam, who'd freed himself from his parents' clutches when he was just eighteen.

"You don't approve," William said, and she shrugged. It really wasn't for her to judge if he should have a prenup or not. In general, she didn't like the idea—there was something mercenary and cynical about preparing for the end of a marriage before it had even started—but was practical enough to know that contracts were necessary when wealth and assets were involved. "I know you think love is supposed to be forever," he continued. "But you know how things are."

"I know," she murmured, not bothering to tell him the reason she disapproved of his actions. If he wanted a prenup, he should own up to it—not blame his father. And if he didn't want one, he should stand up for what he believed in.

"And it's not like how it was with us, you know?" he said, his eyes softening. "I mean, I've only been seeing Penelope for a little over a year."

Warning bells that he might be trying to get back together rang in her head before she remembered that this was William she was talking to. He wasn't actually serious about rekindling their relationship. It was probably just a case of cold feet, coupled with his chronic self-doubt. Belonging to a family filled with overachievers, he'd developed self-esteem issues from constantly comparing himself to them. She'd forgotten that about him and how off-putting it could be.

"Don't make us more than what we really were," she said. "You know we should've broken up long before we did. We were settling for friendship rather than some deep love." She smiled to lessen the blow. "I'm pretty sure I remember hearing about you partying every night after we broke up." His cheeks flamed, and she continued, "You wouldn't have done that if you'd actually felt something for me." And she wouldn't have felt so relieved that he wouldn't be constantly guilting her for not spending enough time with him anymore. Sure, her pride had been hurt when she'd heard how much he was embracing the single life, but it had only been that—her pride. Her heart hadn't even been nicked a little.

"I was young—"

"But honest with yourself," Olivia interrupted. "Let's face it, we were driving each other nuts at the end."

He paused, and she could almost see him remembering the fights.

"William, don't do this," she said. "I mean, you proposed to Penelope, right?" He nodded, albeit reluctantly. "I'm sure you wouldn't have proposed without good—" She froze when Adam appeared at her door.

"It's you again?" he said as he walked into the room. He

murmured a "hello" to her before kissing her, then took the seat next to William, resting his ankle on his knee. "I wonder what your fiancée would say if she knew about all your visits to Olivia."

"Leave Penelope out of this!" William said, and Adam's eyebrows rose.

"Then you better stay away from my girlfriend."

The sudden steel in his voice caused Olivia to jump in. "That's enough, you two." She turned towards William. "I think it's best if we don't see each other for a while."

His eyes widened. "You don't mean that."

"I do, actually. I don't think we can be friends until you realize that we're never getting back together."

"It's because of him, isn't it?" William sneered as he looked at Adam. She was about to deny it when he continued, "You know today isn't the first time he's threatened me. He came to my office, claiming he'd tell Penelope about me wanting us to get back together if I didn't stay away from you."

She blinked, stunned that he would make up such a story. William was a lot of things, but he wasn't a liar. After a moment, she realized that Adam wasn't denying William's claims and felt lead settle in her stomach. He'd deny it if it weren't true, wouldn't he?

Knowing that she could only handle one problem at a time, she focused on William, "I think it best you leave."

"Fine," he said as he straightened. "Call me when you tire of him," he said before he stormed out of the room.

"I'm sorry," Adam said once they were alone. "But you know I was right. He wants you."

Olivia blinked back tears. He didn't get it, did he? "You don't trust me," she said, meeting his gaze.

He cursed as he ran his hand through his hair and gestured towards her. "You said it yourself. You have this connection to him, and he obviously wanted you back. What did you expect me to do? Leave it be?"

"Yes! That's exactly what you should've done." Realizing that their voices had gotten loud, she stood and closed the door. Thankfully, most people had already left for the day. She didn't need an audience. "There was never any risk that I'd leave you for him or cheat," she said as she turned towards him. That wasn't her.

"I know that. I trust you, but I just couldn't help myself, okay?"

"Can you imagine how it'll be when I have to leave town for work? You'd think I was seeing other men the whole time I was gone." Her chest tightened at the truth of her words and she knew that their relationship would never withstand her career changing the way she wanted it to. She'd be out of town for weeks on end.

"That's not true," he said, standing. "I wouldn't—"

"I can't be with someone who's constantly waiting for the other shoe to drop." They were only delaying the inevitable. If she let this pass, he'd just find another way to tear them apart, and frankly, she deserved better. It was best to end things now before she fell even more in love with him.

Because she was in love with him, she numbly realized. Her heart wouldn't feel as if it were breaking into a million tiny pieces right now if she wasn't.

She'd been such a fool. She'd known they didn't have a future. He didn't want children. Hell, he didn't even believe in marriage. But she'd chosen to ignore all that to enjoy the present, and now it was coming to bite her in the ass.

His jaw clenched. "So this is it, then?"

Her throat tightened as she nodded. It had to be.

"All right. I hope you have a good life." He practically spat out the words before leaving.

Once he was gone, she locked her door and gave into the tears she'd been holding back.

# CHAPTER TWENTY-SIX

Adam feigned noninterest as he checked his emails on his phone while his dad flicked through his offer to bail out Dannier. He'd been expecting his dad to bring lawyers and advisors, but when he'd shown up to his office by himself, Adam had decided not to bring anyone into the meeting room, either. It made sense in a way. It was a family matter, so they were keeping it between family.

His dad flipped a page, then cursed. "You really are a bastard, you know that?"

Adam laughed as he looked at the man. "I'm letting you keep a fifteen percent stake of the company. I think that's more than fair at this valuation."

"And kicking me out in the process."

"I am. I don't want to give the people who've run the company into the ground another chance to do so again with my money." His father was undoubtedly angrier about losing access to a company credit card than anything else.

Mom and Dad had both enjoyed a lot of perks at the company's expense and that would end now.

"And the distributions?"

Yeah. Adam was definitely right about that. All Dad cared about was money. "No distributions will be made until long after the company starts seeing a profit and even then, I may choose to reinvest the profits back into the company." After his parents' treatment of his aunt and cousin, he wanted to give them a taste of their own medicine.

His dad's face reddened and Adam laughed. Dad wouldn't still be here if the offer was truly as bad as he was making it out to be. Frankly, Adam doubted his father would've been happy with anything less than full control of the company—something no one in their right mind would give him after everything he'd done.

Given that Adam wasn't even sure he'd get his money back, it was a more than fair offer. But he had to try. Olivia certainly would've if she were in his position. His chest tightened at the thought of her. For what seemed to be the hundredth time, he wondered where she was and what she was doing. He hated not knowing, hated not having the right to know. He knew what he'd done was wrong and understood her reasons for breaking up with him, but he hadn't felt right since. It was as if a big piece of him was missing and only she could make him whole again.

He'd picked up the phone so many times this past week to call her but had never followed through. The fact that he was willing to beg her to give him another chance scared him. He'd never wanted anyone to have that kind of control over him, but somehow, she did. His head knew she was right to end things, but his heart just couldn't accept it. But still, he stayed away. He'd hurt her and knew he'd only hurt her again if she forgave him. He just wasn't built for relationships. He never had been.

"Who will you be putting in charge? Anyone I know?" His dad's voice triggered memories of all the things his parents had put each other through—all in the name of love—and knew Olivia had made the right decision.

Sure, it hurt now, but the pain of goodbye would be worse if they'd continued seeing each other. She might not cheat on him, but they wanted different things in life. Eventually, she'd come to resent him, and as much as he wanted to be with her, having her resent him would just about kill him.

"Alfred Thompson," he said, answering his dad's question, and his dad sputtered.

"That old coot? You're replacing me with him?"

Knowing that he didn't have to explain himself, Adam nodded then pointed at the agreement in front of his father. "That offer isn't going to be there forever, you know." He might not have his personal life in order, but at least his business one was.

* * *

Olivia sighed as she headed to her dad's office with her Yosemite material. He'd called her earlier, saying that he wanted to talk about her proposal. She would've normally been ecstatic at the development, but instead, the numbness that had taken over since she'd ended the relationship with Adam prevailed.

But no matter how much she regretted it, she knew she'd made the right decision. Apart from their differences of views on family, she couldn't be with someone who didn't trust her. Because without trust, what was there?

She hated to think their relationship had just been lust on his end, but she had a sinking feeling that it was. Reminding herself that the hows and whys didn't matter, because the relationship was over, she forced a smile as she walked into her dad's office. She wouldn't let her personal life interfere with work.

"Hi, Dad."

"Hey, sweetie. Take a seat." She did as told and couldn't help but notice his twinkling eyes. "We just bought the site of The Old Lodge," he said, referring to the abandoned hotel in Yosemite she'd suggested they buy for her proposed hotel. "Plus the plot of land next to it."

"Wait? You're approving my Yosemite hotel?" she asked, surprised. She'd thought he would point out issues with her proposal that she'd need to fix before considering it further—not suddenly approve it.

"Yes. I didn't want you to get your hopes up in case our purchase offer was rejected."

"Thank you!" she said as she stood and hugged him. "Wait—how much more land did you buy?" As it was, the property was already big enough to allow for the hiking trails and horseback riding she had planned.

"A little less than six hundred acres."

She stared dumbfounded at her dad. Was he insane?

What were they going to do with six hundred acres? Build a convention center?

"I have a few ideas for the place, including a golf course."

She laughed. Of course he did. He'd picked up golfing while he was recovering from his heart attack and it had stuck. She was unnerved by the sudden realization of just how big an undertaking this was going to be, but at the same time, she was excited that she was finally moving one step closer to her dream of having her own line of hotels.

"Do you think we can use some of my designs?" She'd included quite a few sketches of how she envisioned the buildings and interiors in her proposal, though she'd have to revise them to account for the bigger area. They'd need more guestrooms as well as another restaurant, and possibly even another conference room.

Her dad nodded. "Definitely. I love the rustic feel of it. It's different from our usual fare, but it suits the area." He smiled as he patted her arm. "I'll have James McAllister help you," he said, referring to the person in charge of new developments. "And I'll have Donovan take over your duties with The Mansion."

"I—" She shook her head, speechless. "Thank you so much for believing in me and this project," she said when she finally found her voice. "It really means a lot to me. I know I wasn't much help when we found out Gen Capital was colluding with Parker to fix the books, but I promise to do better this time."

"What are you talking about? I don't know what I

would've done without you. You made sure everything went on without a hitch while I was recovering."

"But I lost us our flagship hotel. I shouldn't have allowed them to make the change from our management to Parker's."

"I would've done the same if I'd been there. And if we'd sued, we probably would've still been stuck with those bastards as partners. I won't say that it didn't hurt to lose the Whitcombe, but we saved ourselves a buttload of trouble in the long run by selling. Have you been feeling guilty all this time?"

"Of course. It wasn't like you to give in. You would've fought tooth and nail if you'd been there."

"I'll admit I hate being made a fool of, but it just wasn't worth it to fight. Gen Capital fought us every single step of the way. Sales were stagnating by that time and the hotel was long overdue for a refresh." He shook his head. "They kept pushing back on talks for a renovation, because of the costs, and I realized that that wasn't how I wanted to run the company. The fact that Mehti is still fighting with them almost two years later after their own problems cemented the knowledge that we made the right decision," he said, referring to another hotel operator Gen Capital had used the same tactic on. "But I'm sorry we never really spoke about it. I would've said something if I'd known you were feeling guilty. At the time, I was just angry that someone had gotten the better of me."

His words eased some of her guilt, though a part of her still couldn't help thinking that it had happened under her watch and for that, she deserved some blame. The fact that he'd chosen to trust her again humbled her and she silently vowed that she wouldn't let him down.

* * *

Adam watched as Alfred and his wife mingled with the Dannier employees. They were announcing the changeover in management today and, to keep up appearances, his parents had organized a small party—as if this were some kind of a retirement party instead of the takeover it was.

He would've preferred something simpler for the announcement, but figured he'd allow his parents to save face. Though there were rumors of the company's hardships, there wasn't anything concrete and he'd rather not feed the flames.

"You can consider yourself out of an inheritance," his mom said as she sidled up next to him and he tamped down the urge to smile. If he had to guess, he'd say that he'd been written out of their will years ago.

"I'll keep that in mind."

Her hand tightened around the champagne flute she was carrying. "You always were an insufferable bastard. Why couldn't you be more like your brother?"

"If I were, this would've been a liquidation sale instead of a retirement party."

"You think robbing your father blind is funny?" she asked as she turned to face him.

"It's not robbing when he brought the company to this." If truth be told, he'd given his parents a better deal than they would've gotten elsewhere. But they were the kind of people who would never be happy with what they had.

"You're so righteous and holy. I can't wait for the day you get taken down a peg." She harrumphed before walking away towards a group of people he didn't recognize.

Shaking his head, Adam looked across the room and saw Denise talking to Alfred in the corner alone. He headed in their direction and, as he neared, he saw that the two were holding hands. Cute.

"Nervous?" he asked Alfred.

"Yeah," Alfred said as he looked around the room. "It's a little weird to see everything so different and yet so similar, but it's good to see so many familiar faces." He smiled as he looked at his wife. "I'm so lucky to have Denise here with me."

Denise blushed as she gently slapped her husband's shoulder. "Oh, you."

"No. It's true," he said as he turned towards Adam. "Life has never been the same since your daddy let me go, but—" He choked up a little before continuing, "She's been with me through thick and thin. I don't know what I would've done without her." He looked adoringly at his wife and Adam couldn't help but think it similar to the way Olivia's dad looked at his wife and the way Luke looked at Samantha.

Tapping on a microphone, his dad called for the room's attention. Adam's gaze scanned the crowd for his mom until he found her making eye contact with one of the waiters on the other side of the room. And he suddenly realized how different their relationship was compared to Alfred and Denise's.

Denise had had Alfred's back through thick and thin and though Mom was here, it was for appearance's sake only—not for moral support. If she were, she wouldn't be flirting with a waiter half her age. While Adam knew that it was just her way of fighting back after Dad's numerous affairs, he couldn't help but feel sorry for them. They'd loved each other once, but all they ever seemed to do now was hurt each other.

His parents' marriage would've never survived what Alfred and Denise had gone through. By supporting each other and being there for one another, Alfred and Denise had made the other stronger, not weaker. The idea seemed crazy, but it made sense. Hadn't he felt stronger when he was with Olivia? Happier? Sure, loving her was a weakness, but the benefits far outweighed the costs.

The people in the room began to clap and he looked up to see Alfred take the stage. Knowing that Alfred had this, he turned to leave. He had to see Olivia.

# CHAPTER TWENTY-SEVEN

Olivia was making a checklist of everything she needed to do on her trip to California next week when her doorbell rang. She checked her phone and was surprised to see Stacy and her bodyguard.

"I'm coming," she said through the app, then went quickly to her door. She opened the door to find her friend carrying a huge bag of food.

"I brought Italian!"

Her heart softened at Stacy's attempt to keep her spirits up. Though Olivia wasn't in the mood to talk about her breakup, she appreciated having a friend who cared so much about her.

"You have wonderful timing. I was just about to order dinner."

"Great! I'll set everything up, and then you can tell me all about your Yosemite plans."

Stacy was basically telling her that she didn't have to talk about Adam if she didn't want to. Olivia didn't know if it was because of that or because of the fact that her friend had gone through something similar, but she broke down on a sob.

"I should've broken up with him when I realized there wasn't a future for us," Olivia said when she finally found her voice. There'd been red flags everywhere, but she'd willfully ignored them. "I fooled myself into believing that I could just enjoy the present, but deep down, I was hoping that I could change his mind."

Stacy ran a hand comfortingly down her back. "Men rarely think about settling down. It's just one of those things that creep up on you."

"But I should've heeded the signs. No matter how perfect a boyfriend he was, we didn't want the same things. If that's not a recipe for disaster, I don't know what is."

"I know William can be an ass sometimes, but I still can't believe Adam thought you were cheating on him with William. Seriously."

"And that he felt the need to threaten William! As if I couldn't control myself around the man."

"It means that he cares about you."

"But it's not enough." Yes, he cared about her, but he didn't trust her one whit. "I guess I should be thankful that William's visit showed Adam's true colors before I fell any deeper in love with him, but I just feel so drained right now." She'd finally gotten everything that she'd ever wanted—The Mansion back in the family fold, her own hotel… But she still wasn't happy, and it was all because of Adam.

"I'm so sorry, honey," Stacy said as she hugged her.

"I'm sure it'll get better in time," Olivia lied, more to herself than to her friend. She'd felt almost nothing after she and William broke up, but now, she felt as if she were dying inside. She wasn't sure if she'd ever get better. Olivia forced a smile as she grabbed her friend's hand. "Thanks for coming."

"Of course, though we better eat before the food gets cold." They headed towards the dining table and Olivia went to clean up all the work she'd left there.

"Hold on. I want to take a look at everything," Stacy said, referring to the sketches and floor plans Olivia had spread out.

Stacy laughed as she took it in. "You have everything set up."

"I've had a lot of time to think about it," Olivia murmured as she looked at the sketch of the lobby. She was just thinking about how seamless the check-in experience would be from the moment a guest arrived at the hotel when she frowned. She'd spent more time working on the design of the hotel than she had on the actual business proposal.

She'd thought she'd gotten over her dreams of being an architect, but the fact that she'd even included these elaborate concept designs and floor plans in her proposals proved that false. She'd told herself that drawing everything out made her see and understand things better, but the truth was that she loved designing and had been trying to find a way to combine that passion with her work at Montgomery.

By including designs in her proposals, she'd been doing

the parts she enjoyed—the imagining and the drawing. Whether intentional or not, by only showing her designs to a select few, she'd ended up avoiding criticism.

It didn't escape her notice that it had been the criticism in Studio that she'd struggled with the most with in college. She'd always loved designing but trying to incorporate everyone's feedback had been pure torture. She'd spend hours trying to improve her designs—often even longer than she'd spent on the original design, and it still hadn't been enough.

She couldn't help but think of Seth, who'd also had a hard time at school. But instead of dropping out, he'd persisted. She'd never considered herself a coward, but she'd acted like one in this respect. She'd struggled in school and had left as soon as an opportunity for something different—something easier—arose. What's worse was that she'd never seriously considered going back to finish her studies after her father recovered. She'd told herself that her dreams had changed when in reality, she'd been afraid of failure.

"I've been so blind," she murmured.

"Huh?"

"I told myself that I didn't want to pursue a career in architecture, but I was still designing every chance I got. I've never really let go of my dreams. I just suppressed them. Badly."

Stacy laughed. "You were enjoying working with your family, so it wasn't like it was all bad."

"I took the easy road," Olivia said as she shook her head. But she wouldn't any longer. "I'll finish this project, then go back to school," she suddenly decided. She didn't want to look back years from now and have any regrets.

* * *

Olivia had just stepped out of the shower when her doorbell rang.

Wondering who could be visiting at this hour, she checked her phone and was surprised to see Adam. While a part of her wanted to ignore him, another part drank in the sight of him. She'd missed him.

"I'll be out in a minute," she said as she donned a robe, then went downstairs, her mind in a whirl. Was he here to apologize? Did she want him to apologize?

She opened the door and they stared wordlessly at each other. It seemed forever before he broke the silence. "May I come in?"

Her throat tight, she nodded as she stepped back.

"I'm really sorry for the way I acted," he said once he was inside. "I know it doesn't seem like it, but I do trust you." He shook his head. "I've always thought love was a weakness—a tool someone could use against you. When I realized I was falling for you, I panicked. I've never felt this way before and it scared me, so I pushed you away. And then when I saw William—" He sighed. "If I'd been thinking straight, I would've known that you'd never go behind my back. But I guess some part of me worried that he'd be willing to give you what I couldn't." He grabbed hold of her hands and clasped them together with his. "But

I'm not afraid anymore. The only thing I'm afraid of is losing you. I love you."

Her heart rose. "You love me?"

Earnest eyes looked at her as he cupped her face. "I do. I can't promise that I won't get jealous again, because I know that wouldn't be true, but I promise that I'll always trust you and never go behind your back again."

She blinked back tears. "I love you, too." Happiness filled her before reality set in. How would he feel about her working in California? "Oh! I never told you—my dad approved my Yosemite proposal."

"Congratulations," he said, beaming as he hugged her. "I knew you could do it." Before she could voice her concerns about being stationed so far away, he said, "And I'll support you in anything that you do. If that means following you to wherever you're building a hotel, then I'll do it."

Her heart softened and she kissed him. "It'll only be for this one hotel," she explained as they broke away. "Afterwards, I'll go back to school." She shook her head. "All this time, I had told myself that I'd gotten over my dreams and was happy working with the family, but in reality, I was afraid of failure."

"That better be architecture school you're talking about," he said, and she laughed.

"It is."

"Then I support you one hundred percent. I know it wasn't an easy decision, but I'm glad that you've decided to follow your dreams. With your sense of design, I know you'll be an amazing architect."

Her cheeks warmed. "Thank you."

"I probably shouldn't admit this, but as much as I hate you doubting yourself, I'm happy that you stuck in Montgomery longer than you should've, because it brought you to me."

"We would've probably met at the grand opening of the hotel."

"Perhaps, but then I wouldn't have gotten to work with you and get to know you the way I did."

"That might've been a good thing. With me trying to preserve so much of my grandfather's vision, I can't imagine I was easy to work with."

"You definitely weren't what I was expecting, but I really enjoyed working with you. Your passion for the hotel was downright contagious, and I found myself looking at things in a completely different light."

Sighing, she kissed him. He said the sweetest things.

His eyes darkened as he fingered her robe. "You're naked underneath this, aren't you?"

Laughing, she nodded, and he groaned. Excitement unfurled in her stomach as she grabbed his hands. "Come on," she said as she led him down the hall.

They had just stepped into the bedroom when he pulled her towards him and kissed her.

"I've missed you," he said as he palmed her face.

"I've missed you, too," she murmured before he kissed her again.

Biting her lip, he pulled away and untied the sash of her robe, his eyes soaking in her naked body. "Lie down," he said gruffly.

A thrill shot through her at his words and she did just that. He covered her body with his, kissing her until she was breathless. He peppered kisses down the column of her throat before nibbling on the sensitive spot at the base of her neck, sending waves of pleasure coursing through her.

Needing to touch him, she began unbuttoning his shirt. Groaning, he sat up and removed his shirt, revealing his toned muscles before coming back down to her. She welcomed him with open arms, enjoying the feel of his hard strength as she ran her hands all over him.

Wetness pooled between her legs as he laved a nipple, circling it with his tongue, driving her insane. Needing him now, she rolled over him and reached for his belt. She quickly undid his pants and pulled them down, along with his boxers.

A delicious thrill rose inside of her when he guided her down his cock, their moans mingling in the air. She placed her hands on his chest and moved, taking delight in the way he watched her.

"You're so hot," Adam said as he teased her clit, sending her nerve endings haywire. Wanting to drive him crazy as well, she rode him faster. It wasn't long before her muscles began contracting around him and she flew apart.

Groaning, he rolled over her, lifted her leg over his shoulder, and picked up the pace. Sensation after sensation poured through her as he hit just the right spot, and she soon found herself at the edge again.

"Come with me," he said, and she did, the pleasure so intense she cried out with it.

## CHAPTER TWENTY-EIGHT

Olivia bit her lip as she approached her father's office Monday morning. Hopefully, he wouldn't be too disappointed when she told him about her plans to return to school.

She'd always known he wanted one of his children to take over his duties at Montgomery and while she'd enjoyed working here, it had more to do with the fact that she was working on the family's legacy as opposed to actually enjoying the work she did.

And while she didn't regret the time she spent here, she wished she'd come to her realization sooner—before her father had spent millions on the Yosemite plot. She still wanted to see the project through but would understand if he chose to scrap the project altogether. Dad liked to dream big and a one-off hotel with a different focus just might not be worth the effort.

She knocked on the door and her dad beamed. "Olivia! Come in!" he said as he motioned her inside. "How're your preparations for the trip going?" he asked, referring to her trip to Yosemite later this week.

His obvious excitement only made her feel worse. She'd pushed him so hard to approve one of her proposals and now that he'd actually bought the land, she decided she didn't want to work at the company anymore?

Not wanting to get his hopes up any more than she already had, she suddenly blurted, "I've decided to go back to school." His smile disappeared and she quickly added, "I'd still love to be in charge of the project or to work in any capacity if you decide to move forward with the hotel." Not only did she not want to leave anything unfinished, she'd also fallen in love with her concept and wanted to be the one to bring it to life. "But it would just be a one-off thing and not the mini-chain I'd originally been planning. I'm sorry."

Dad sighed. "You have nothing to apologize about. I guess it's a miracle you stayed this long. I've always known you wanted to be an architect, but I thought that helping with all the renovations as the relations manager would be enough to satisfy the designer in you."

"It did to some extent, but I want to design more than just occasionally. And when I do, I don't want to hand off the project to an architect because I don't have the neces-sary skills."

"I should've realized that it wouldn't be enough. Are you sure you want to continue with the Yosemite hotel? I wouldn't blame you if you didn't want to. You've already done so much for me and the company. I know I've said it many times, but I don't know what I would've done without you. Knowing that you were at the office while I was at home, recuperating, gave me peace of mind so that I could focus on my health."

"Getting to work with you was my favorite part about this job, which I think is why I stayed so long. And I do want to continue working on the project. After dreaming about it for so long, it feels like my baby."

"I know what you mean. I can still remember when I built my first hotel." He thought about it for a minute, then nodded. "If that's really how you feel, then we'll go on with the project with you in charge. It's an expensive experiment to test the waters, but if there really is a demand here with these adventurer hotels, we would be the first to capitalize on it in big ways."

He wasn't mad at her.

Olivia sighed in relief as her dad began talking about how their customer base was getting younger and younger and how hotels like this one could set Montgomery apart from their competitors. She'd been worried sick about talking to him all weekend and here he was, talking about how her concept could potentially grow Montgomery's business.

Her dad was simply amazing, and she gave a quick, silent prayer of thanks for having such a wonderful family.

* * *

*Would the two businessmen ever leave?*

Adam inwardly groaned as he took another sandwich from the three-tiered stand to stall. Since Olivia didn't like to bring attention to herself, he'd originally wanted to close down The Mansion's tearoom for his proposal. But then, she'd know something was up. He'd finally settled on going later in the evening and closing the restaurant early, so that by the time he proposed, the place would be empty.

He'd had it all planned out in his head—the modified tea presentation (it was normally served as a buffet in the afternoons,) the fairy lights that the waiter would turn on as soon they'd been served their dessert stand, the proposal... But what he hadn't planned for were the two customers a few tables down who seemed content to talk all night. He guessed he could ask for the dessert to be brought out and just wait for the businessmen to leave before he proposed, but how would he get the message across to the waiter?

He was contemplating his options when the waiter came. "How is everything going? Are you ready for dessert?"

"Yes," he said as he shook his head, hoping that Edgar got the message. "Thank you."

"Is everything all right?" Olivia asked once the waiter left.

"Yeah. Why?"

She laughed. "Because you just said yes while you were shaking your head. And you've been looking at those men practically the whole evening. Do you know them?"

"I'll tell you about it later." He smiled. "Did you enjoy the meal?"

"I loved it! It was such a great idea to dine here before they start remodeling." Olivia then started talking about how she hadn't been here for tea since her grandparents had taken her as a child.

As they were eating cake twenty minutes later, the two businessmen stood, and he breathed a sigh of relief. Finally! Once they were gone, he sought the eyes of the waiter and nodded.

The restaurant's lights dimmed and a second later, the decorative lights turned on. Olivia's eyes widened as she looked around, and he got the box from his pocket. He stood, then bent down on one knee.

"Olivia Anne Montgomery, would you do me the honor of becoming my wife? We won't be making any lists of the richest couples anytime soon, but we'd never want for anything."

A part of him had wanted to wait until Dannier was profitable before he proposed—until he was a little more financially stable—but he couldn't wait to marry her. After realizing that he wanted to spend the rest of his life with her, he didn't want to waste another moment without her. Hopefully, she felt the same.

"I'd love to," she said as she wrapped her arms around him and kissed him. "And I don't care about the other stuff," she said as she pulled away. "I mean, I want you to succeed in all you do, but if not, we'll still be good because we have each other, right?"

His heart swelled with love. He didn't think he could love her any more, but he did, and he made a promise to himself that he'd never let her regret her decision. "Right," he said, smiling before he kissed her.

Two Years Later

"Let's make sure we leave by ten," Adam told her as they walked into the newly designed Mansion, and Olivia smiled. Adam had been extra protective of her ever since they'd found out she was pregnant. It was a little earlier than they'd originally planned on having children, but they were thrilled.

"Okay." Since she had school the next day, she was more than okay with the plan.

She'd enrolled after she'd stepped down from overseeing the construction of the Yosemite hotel. She hadn't liked the thought of traveling so much and overseeing a construction site while she was pregnant.

Her father had offered her an advisory role and she'd quickly accepted. She loved the fact that she'd get to have a continuing role in shaping the future of her first and only hotel. Depending on how things went, Dad was already thinking about opening a location in Sedona.

"And if you start to feel any pain, let me know," Adam said, and she smiled. It was easy to see that he already loved the baby. On top of taking extra care of her, he'd made the difficult decision to completely cut his parents out of his life. He hadn't wanted their toxic behavior anywhere near the baby.

Considering how much her own parents meant to her, Olivia had felt bad about it, but after the way Adam's siblings had shown support for his decision, she figured they knew more about the subject than she did.

"They really did an amazing job," Adam said as he looked around the lobby, and she agreed. The renovation had far exceeded her expectations. Elegant and modern, the new design kept the spirit of the original Mansion alive in a way that was sure to delight for generations to come. Grandpa would've loved it. Adam squeezed her hand as he added, "But then again, I'm partial because it's the reason we met."

"Aww, you." Olivia kissed him. "Here, I want to show you the bar," she said as she pulled him towards the bar. It was brand new, but the rich wood paneling and design made it timeless. She could easily imagine her grandfather taking a seat and ordering a drink there. "I'm so jealous I didn't get to work more on the hotel."

"Maybe on the next remodeling," Adam said, and she laughed.

Perhaps.

## AUTHOR'S NOTE

Thanks so much for reading *Business Before Pleasure!* I hope you enjoyed it. To hear about my new releases, sign up for my mailing list at natashagrace.com

# UNSPOKEN DESIRES

After finding out that her husband had been cheating on her, the only thing recently widowed Samantha Collins wants to do is to put her old life behind her. The first thing on the checklist? To sell her husband's share of the hedge fund he started with his best friend.

Only Luke Darren has different plans.

More comfortable with running the day-to-day operations of the firm, Luke has always stayed in the background, letting Jason become the face of the company. But now that Jason's gone, clients have been leaving in droves. The last thing he needs is for Samantha to leave as well. It would be the last straw for the customers who were already on the fence about pulling their money out and Luke couldn't risk that.

But soon, working with Samantha is wrecking his concentration. He's been in love with her for years and with Jason no longer in the way, being friends just isn't enough and he soon finds himself wanting more!